The Coesen

SHEA SWAIN

Other Books Written By:

Shea Swain
The Pulse of Provocative Romance

What Lilly Wants
An Erotic Novella

INVIDIOUS Betrayal
A Full-Length Paranormal-Sci Romance

ABSOLVE
A Short Romantic New Adult Drama

Winter's Icy Heart
A Short Romantic Contemporary

Chained to the Devil's Son
A Full-Length Dark Romance

The Binding of the Halo Series
Four Full-Length Paranormal Romance Series
The Binding of the Halo Book I
The Awakening of the Halo Book II
The Descent of the Halo III
The Battle for the Halo IIII

Heaven on Hell Island
A Full-Length Enemies to Lovers Romance

Prologue

A whisper in the air caught Arkean's attention but the sensation of something touching his arm caused him to move into a crouched position and ready to strike. The fine hairs on his neck stood up and his stomach buzzed with nervous energy as he stared out into the darkness.

As far as he knew, no one was inside the cave except him and his brethren who slept just inches away. Yet, Arkean was sure he heard someone calling out. The words were foreign to him but the tone suggested it was a call for help.

"Wake up," Arkean said, shaking the leg of each of his companions.

Bode got to his feet instantly, ready for whatever the threat was.

Quende and Gedgi were slower to wake but after a few seconds they were up on their feet. Each looking over their shoulders with wide questioning eyes.

"What is it?" Bode asked, whispering.

"Do you not hear that?" Arkean responded, quietly. "Someone's calling out for help."

"Are you crazed, Arkean?" Quende asked as he rub sleep from his eyes.

Bode covered Quende's mouth with his hand, "*Shhh-hush*. Listen. I hear it too."

As the others visibly strained to hear what Arkean and Bode clearly heard, Arkean continued to scan the cave from where he stood. After a few quiet minutes, Arkean looked back to Gedgi who's eyes widened as he gasped.

"What is that?" Gedgi asked as he peered around the dark cave.

The moon provided some light but not enough for them to see in every crevice and corner.

"So, you hear it?" Arkean didn't think the call for help was coming from outside so he took a step toward the darkest part of the cave where he found a small opening when scouting earlier. It was barely wide enough for him to squeeze through so he didn't think much of it at the time.

Bode held his arm out, blocking Arkean from moving forward. "Wait," he whispered. "That doesn't sound like any language I know. We do not know what waits beyond that opening."

Quende stepped up. "We are almost home. She we…"

"Whatever it is, it is in pain," Arkean said, as he gently pushed his cousin's hand away. "It calls to us for help. I cannot ignore a call for help from man or animal, Bode."

1

A New Path

Circa 556 B.C.,

The continent of Africa, eighteen days ago.

Sweat trickled under Arkean's jaw and down his neck. He brushed away another bead of sweat from his brow that dropped to his shoulder as he scanned his surroundings. His countrymen were close behind, each looking around. Their brows were wet as well but the Sun and all its glory was a part of them, of who they were. The stifling heat was of no consequence.

To the Bodai, the sun was life and strength. It marked time and provided light to them. Arkean thanked the Gods for the gift of the Sun and all it bestowed on him and his kin. The heat was a slight annoyance and nothing more. A less than fair trade for all the Sun provided them. Even now, as Arkean trekked through the rough terrain of the desert, the Sun's rays were relentless in their assault but none of the four warriors complained.

Arkean looked over at Bode, who was several paces ahead and was now squatting, looking around for the threat they all seemed to have sensed. Bode suddenly dropped into a defensive stance in the waist high grass.

Arkean, Quende, and Gedgi followed Bode's lead. With a series of hand signals, the young men communicated what the threat was and their intended response.

The three watched quietly as Bode scanned the vast expanse that took seven rising suns to reach from their village. This wasn't their land but it was familiar to them. Many of their generations recited epic tales about the same path they were walking, so they had an idea of what dangers awaited.

Arkean saw Bode raise his hand and signaled them to be ready. All four young men silently strung their bows as they remained crouched down then faced off in different directions. Looking out over the territory he sentried, Arkean tightened his hand over the smooth center arc of his weapon.

Each bow was crafted by its owner and considered a capable weapon that every Bodai male trained with diligently from the moment of its creation until their skill was perfected. Each warrior wielded his with deadly accuracy.

Arkean scanned his area thoroughly, knowing his brethren to do the same. He trusted each of them with his life and they trusted him. That trust would serve them well during the journey.

All Bodai youth who chose the warrior's path had to travel from their village through harsh inhospitable lands as a rite of passage. Their mission was to survive on their own until their tasks were completed, after which they returned home as Guardians, protectors of their people.

Alert, Arkean focused on the tall muscled warrior passing by. From the markings on the man's body, he knew the man was a warrior from a warring tribe who had a village nearby. Arkean knew the high dry grass hid him and his friends well but his muscles tensed as he silently drew back his bowstring.

The warrior kept a lazy pace as he sang, never stalling or giving a glance in their direction. Still, they waited several tense minutes after he passed before relaxing. They waited another few minutes to make certain he was alone before continuing their way.

The village the warrior was from was a compound of warmongers. The Bodai elders often shared tales of the warriors' bloodthirsty invasions and how they were bent on conquering lands beyond their borders. Their bodies seemed to be bred for battle, were large in number, and were known to be uncompromising, unfriendly, and belligerent.

The Bodai were the complete opposites. Their men and women chose roles that provided for each member of their community in different ways. Some farmed the land, some raised the young, some governed.

The COESEN

Arkean, Bodai, Quende, and Gedgi decided early on in their lives that they were warriors. Each of them endured the strenuous training required and prepared their bodies and minds as warriors to become Guardians of their tribe.

Even though the Warmonger's were bent on conquering, they stayed away from the Bodai's village due to a long-standing agreement. But encroaching on their land was forbidden. That is why their first challenge was passing the warmongering village.

It was dangerous and because of that, it was where the journey began and ended for some of Arkean's brethren. Getting around the warmonger's village unseen was the smart way and it was how the four agreed to accomplish the task when they decided to partner in this journey, known as the Maatii.

After passing the borders of the warmonger' village, Quende and Gedgi secured their bows over their bodies and easily fell into their usual free-spirited ways. Gedgi and Quende laughed quietly about something. The two were only fifteen Sumas or dry seasons old. They were still quite youthful and responsibilities hadn't weighed their spirits down too much.

Arkean looked at Quende as they walk. He was of average height, had dark brown skin, deep-set eyes, and shoulder length dark brown hair that he kept in several braids tied with black leather string. Two deep dimples punctured his cheeks, reminding those who faced off with the strong capable fighter that a boy still lived inside him. He bore many scars on his chest and arms but he wore them proudly because he earned them protecting his sister from their father who tried to force himself on her.

His father didn't survive the encounter.

Gedgi was the shortest of the four. His hair was light brown and shoulder length. His features were softer, almost feminine, and he was the fastest of the four when it came to running or other athletic pursuits.

Bode secured his weapon as he looked around. Arkean eventually secured his weapon by swinging the bow over his head and resting the bowstring on his chest as well. Due to their close relation as cousins, their skin tone was shades lighter than the others. Their hair was the blackest of black; both had long noses and chiseled facial features due to their grandmother, who came from a great empire in the north that sat beside the great river. Unlike Bode who kept his hair in thin adorn braids that were pulled into a single long braid that hung to the middle of his back, Arkean chose to keep his hair short and cropped close to the scalp.

Other difference was that Bode had only seen sixteen sumas and as the son of the King was expected to ascend to the throne. Arkean, having lived through seventeen sumas, was the eldest of the group and that gave him a sense of responsibility even though the others started training before him.

"When do we eat?" Gedgi asked as he high stepped through the dry grass.

Arkean grimaced. They all knew the fear Gedgi had of snakes was due to an incident when he was a young child. Arkean took his friend's fear seriously so he moved in front of Gedgi after motioning for the others to protect their friend on all sides. If there was a snake hiding in the grass, hopefully, he, Bode or Quende would feel it first.

"Let's hunt then find shelter," Bode said.

It was more than a suggestion to them even though Bode's tone was laidback when the words were spoken.

"I'll hunt," Arkean said, looking over his shoulder at Quende and Gedgi. "You all go find shelter. I will track you when done."

His friends gave him a nod but Arkean noticed Bode frowning. His kin made no move to follow the others.

"I will be careful. You do the same," Arkean said as he placed his hand over Bode's chest where his heart beat.

"I will," Bode said, as he placed his hand over Arkean's heart. He gave Arkean a slight smile before running to catch up with the others who waited a short distance away.

●

The sun rose and set eight times before the four approached their second challenge. "We're almost there," Bode called as he ran toward the water.

Arkean kept his pace and was ever watchful as the river came into view. He looked around, knowing that this was the place in all the elders' tales. Quende and Gedgi ran to catch up with his cousin.

"Relax Arkean," Bode shouted when Arkean met them at the shore. Bode dipped his hand in the cool water, cupped some of the liquid, and threw it.

The cool water that splashed over Arkean was welcomed, considering the heat, but unlike the others, he was not in a playful mood.

"He does not know how to relax," Gedgi teased.

Arkean said nothing in his defense. He just peered at Gedgi as Bode forced the kid under the surface of the water.

"Leave Arkean be," Quende said, "One of us has to have a level head." He treaded through the shallow pool until he reached the large rock in the water that led to their second challenge, the river.

Bode and Gedgi stopped playing around and followed.

Raising himself up on extended arms, Quende back kicked water at Bode and Gedgi before climbing out. Bode and Gedgi called out playful threats but Quende ignored them, shook the excess water off, then checked his gear.

Arkean was the last to wade through the cold shallow pool. Wasting no time in the water to cool off, he hoisted himself up on the rock next to Quende and checked that he had his arrows and that his sharpened blade was secured on his hip. As Quende helped Bode and Gedgi out of the pool, Arkean made sure the leather ties of his foot coverings were secure.

While the other two checked their gear, Arkean looked at the only course they could take—a path of rock steps that were in the raging part of the river. The slippery path went on farther than his eyes could see.

"Looks fun," Quende said sarcastically.

Gedgi looked up from his gear. "Who's going first?"

Arkean placed his foot on the first stone step which was very close to where he stood on the islet. He grimaced as he moved forward. "I'll go first," he volunteered.

"I'll go next, then you Gedgi. Quende, you bring up the rear," Bode said as he stepped on the stone Arkean was on, just as Arkean hopped to the next with ease.

The stones were slicker than Arkean thought and the distance between each stone grew further and further apart but the water was still lower than each, allowing them to cross without having to worry about the current.

Winded and with only a few stones remaining until they reach the other side, Arkean realized the water level had risen. He also saw that the current on this part of the river was so strong that he knew if either of them fell in, they would be carried down the river and need to start across again.

They were all exhausted by the time they reached land, but Arkean was relieved that they all made it. They decided to rest for a short while to allow the burning in their thighs to ease before finding shelter. But Arkean's relief was short-lived— their next task would be the most dangerous.

●

It took them several more sunsets until they found the pride of lions. The pride was the reason for their journey. The boys were to bring back the pelt of a lion to show their elders that they were men.

For obvious reasons, none of them wanted to confront the entire pride, so they observed the lions for a few suns to determine the pride's movements. They were always careful to stay downwind of the pride and to watch for rogue males.

Watching and discussing their next moves, they initially decided to wait along the border of the pride's land until the time when the lead lion scented its territory.

Opportunity was the key to their success on this journey and as luck would have it, they didn't have to wait long for a solitary lion. On the third day, just a mile from where they camped, Bode sighted a rogue lion who seemed to be following the pride, but not very closely. He was most likely scavenging for scraps left over.

It is as if great-mother's Sun God is smiling down on us with favor, Arkean thought.

After he alerted the rest of his team, they watched the rogue and hatched their plan. None of the four wanted to be near the pride's territory longer than they had to. Quende volunteered to be the bait, and once their plan was finalized he backed away from the rest of them to get into position. In the meantime, Arkean, Bode, and Gedgi stealthily moved into position to pounce.

Just as they'd planned, the lion took the bait. Quende led the rogue straight into their path. Bode released an arrow, pulled another, and was stringing it to release well before the lion even sensed it was in danger. Both arrows hit the body of the lion but the beast seemed unaffected and aggressively sprinted toward Quende, who was stringing an arrow as he ran.

The beast must have been without food for weeks to take them on after being injured.

Three more arrows from Arkean, Gedgi, and Quende hit the beast in unison. Its front legs buckled and its large head slammed to the ground only a few feet from Quende. Bode and Gedgi immediately turned around, reloading their bows and refocusing their attention to their surroundings for the possibility of any other threats. Arkean and Quende did the same. After a few tense minutes, Bode and Arkean relaxed their bows and closed in on their kill.

Gedgi followed, walking backward as he kept a keen eye on their surroundings. "Alone?" he asked, glancing over his shoulder.

"Alone," Bode replied as he kicked their kill.

Arkean walked around the dying animal to peer out over the expanse of the terrain. "Doesn't mean we should idle." He crouched rubbed over the animal's fur until he felt where his heartbeat was strong then stuck his blade through to the hilt but didn't pull it free.

Bode pulled the arrows free, handing them off to their owners, then Gedgi and Quende lifted their kill and hung it over Arkean's shoulders. Quende supported the rear end while Bode kept his bow strung to guard them.

"Let's get back to the cave. There is a nearby body of water we can use when we skin him," Arkean said.

Bode led the way while Gedgi guarded from behind.

The parts of the lion were to be used in various ways, ceremonial and otherwise. It was important that the boys prepare the remains properly for transportation and eventual use. The lion's mane would be fashioned into a crown for Bode to wear when he became king, so Arkean took his time washing the treasure thoroughly. The skin of the lion would be used to create decorative or useful items for the boys.

Some of the organs would be used as pouches and the teeth and claws would make weapons and jewelry for them or whomever they chose. Some of the meat and organs would be preserved, while some would be eaten now and, on the way back to the village. Some parts were burned as the boys gave thanks to the spirits of their ancestors and prayed for the lion's soul.

As Arkean laid out the skin near the cave wall to dry, he quietly listened to his friends talking.

"When we get back home Bode," Quende said as he chewed his cooked meat, "are you going to claim Eyet?"

Arkean couldn't see his cousin's face but he felt Bode's eyes on his back. The feeling of being watched didn't last long and ended when he heard Bode clear his throat.

"I do not wish to speak of Eyet," Bode finally said.

Arkean was thankful that Bode loved him enough not to discuss his union with Eyet. For that consideration Arkean was grateful, but the simple fact that Bode will claim Eyet caused an ache in Arkean's heart that will forever remain. And there was nothing Arkean could do about it.

He finished what he was doing and took a deep breath before joining his friends. Sitting beside his cousin he distracted himself with thoughts of the stories Cire, his great-mother, told him. He thought of one story in particular—the one of how her people became such a big part of the Bodai.

Long before Cire was born, Matot, a warrior and prince of the Bodai tribe, went to visit the fair-skinned Egyptians to trade and learn their ways. The Egyptians were known far and wide for their arts, building crafts, and form of government. While there, Matot prevented the murder of the king's only son and the abduction of his daughters by an invading tribe.

As thanks, the great king gave one of his daughters to Matot to mate and forged an alliance with him. Matot returned to the Bodai with his mate, and when his father died, Matot became king of the Bodai. Matot was a direct forefather of Arkean and Bode.

Because of continuous strife and wars, the Egyptians experienced during that time, they welcomed the alliance with the Bodai Tribe. The old kings of the Great River, who called themselves Pharaohs, were so impressed by the Bodai Guardians' strength, mind, and determination that they have since sent a royal daughter for every prince in line of succession to the Bodai throne. In return, the Egyptians were given a contingent of Guardians warriors as trade.

The traditional exchange ended long ago and for a time no Egyptian princesses were sent to the Bodai. Then, fifty Sumas ago, Cire was presented to Prince Kire of the Bodai, who already had three wives. Kire ascended to the throne and sent twenty trained Guardians, jewels, and other gifts to the Egyptians as thanks for his new young bride.

Arkean thought of the vast and beautiful place near the great river that used to be his home. He no longer remembered Egypt, the place of his birth or his parents, but his great mother told him many stories that sparked his imagination.

Kire, his grandfather, had three sons with his other wives but they each met tragic ends. With Cire he fathered two more sons and a daughter. Their eldest son, Obade, would later father Bode, and their youngest Dwar fathered Arkean.

As the youngest son of Kire, Dwar had no hope for the title of king of the Bodai, so he went to his mother's land to find his purpose in life. In that land, Dwar proved his worth to his maternal kin, the Pharaoh. Dwar became one of the finest and most decorated soldiers in the Egyptian military. Dwar was so favored he earned the presiding king's favor, friendship, ear, and one of his daughters.

Dwar, a warrior, was rarely home with his wife, who genuinely loved him; but when he was home he treated his delicate young bride like the princess she was. She bore him a son while he was away on a campaign, but he never made it home to rejoice with her. Dwar was betrayed by his men who were bribed by the Pharaoh's brother and planned his death because of his loyalty to the Pharaoh.

With Dwar out of the way, those men, under the command of the Pharaoh's brother, managed to murder most of the royal family including Arkean's mother, to gain the throne. Arkean was just four Sumas old when he was returned to the Bodai as a good faith offer to preserve the alliance with King Kire.

"There was no reason for the Egyptians to kill you, Arkean", Cire told him when he was old enough to understand. "Under the law of my forefathers, no Bodai could ever ascend to the Pharaoh's throne by union or birth. However, your father was a physical threat and a formidable one that the

Pharaoh's brother could not ignore. So, he and your mother were killed."

Though Arkean didn't remember his parents, whenever Cire spoke of their murder, there was a sadness in her voice that made Arkean want to weep.

Nevertheless, the new Pharaoh wanted to maintain an accord with the Bodai, thus his good faith gift of returning Arkean thirteen Sumas ago. Two Sumas ago, Eyet was sent by her father the Pharaoh to reestablish the terms of the old agreement between the two nations. Though still angered about the murder of their kin, sending Eyet back would be an insult to her and her father. Eyet's father was a treacherous Pharaoh but the Bodai had come to treasure the long-held alliance and they did not want to anger the formidable Egyptians.

As the eldest son of the king of the Bodai, Bode was expected to mate with Eyet.

How ironic is it that I desire the daughter of the very man who took my parents from me? Arkean thought as he plucked at his shoe ties.

"Your silence doesn't worry me but the look on your face does, cousin," Bode said. When Arkean didn't respond, Bode handed him a piece of meat. "We saved the best of our meat for you brother."

When Arkean looked at him to inquire why, his cousin smiled.

"You carried the heaviest part of the beast the entire way, diminishing your strength. You also skinned and cut the meat. It is only fair that you enjoy the best parts."

Arkean nodded in thanks as he took his portion and ate.

Bode was going to be a fair and good king. That made it impossible for Arkean to feel any ill feelings toward Bode, even though he would be mating with the woman Arkean loved above all others, above even himself.

Arkean prided himself for being fair and good as well and he could never hate his kin. Hate and jealousy ruined nations. It ruined families. It ruined his.

Even though Cire cared for him and loved him, Arkean knew he reminded her of his father, her slain son, and it haunted him. He saw the pain in her eyes when he unknowingly did something like his father, the man he never knew.

Often, he wished he could be his father for her. She lost her husband Kire to illness and though she had her sister wives—all Kire's sons except for Obade had died in either battle or illness—Arkean sensed that she never recovered from the way she lost Dwar.

When he was returned to the Bodai tribe, everyone accepted Arkean without prejudice, and he found a kinship with his cousin Bode. The two had become as tight as loving brothers. Arkean knew Bode would be king someday and he vowed to train hard and excel in combat because he wanted to protect his king. There weren't many things he knew about his father but Arkean knew his father was loyal to his king and he was proud to say that he was too.

He thought that no one, not even Eyet, knew about his feelings for her, but now Arkean wasn't so sure. Bode may have an idea, which meant that Arkean needed to bury his feelings deep and find a mate he could be happy with.

As a royal, he would have his choice of the finest women in their village. It was going to be hard to welcome another in his heart but he was strong and his mind was sound.

Arkean finished his meat then stood. He sat down at the entrance of the cave to take first watch, infused with a new-found determination.

2

New Acquaintances

Present

A whisper in the air caught Arkean's attention but the sensation of something touching his arm caused him to move into a crouched position and ready to strike. The fine hairs on his neck stood up and his stomach buzzed with nervous energy as he stared out into the darkness.

As far as he knew, no one was inside the cave except him and his brethren who slept just inches away. Yet, Arkean was sure he heard someone calling out. The words were foreign to him but the tone suggested it was a call for help.

"Wake up," Arkean said, shaking the leg of each of his companions.

Bode got to his feet instantly, ready for whatever the threat was.

Quende and Gedgi were slower to wake but after a few seconds, they were up on their feet. Each looking over their shoulders with wide questioning eyes.

"What is it?" Bode asked, whispering.

"Do you not hear that?" Arkean responded, quietly. "Someone's calling out for help."

"Are you crazed, Arkean?" Quende asked as he rubbed the sleep from his eyes.

Bode covered Quende's mouth with his hand, "*Shhh-* hush. Listen. I hear it too."

As the others visibly strained to hear what Arkean and Bode clearly heard, Arkean continued to scan the cave from where he stood. After a few quiet minutes, Arkean looked back to Gedgi who's eyes widened as he gasped.

"What is that?" Gedgi asked as he peered around the dark cave.

The moon provided some light but not enough for them to see in every crevice and corner.

"So, you hear it?" Arkean didn't think the call for help was coming from outside so he took a step toward the darkest part of the cave where he found a small opening when scouting earlier. It was barely wide enough for him to squeeze through so he didn't think much of it at the time.

Bode held his arm out, blocking Arkean from moving forward. "Wait," he whispered. "That doesn't sound like any language I know. We do not know what waits beyond that opening."

Quende stepped up. "We are almost home. She we…"

"Whatever it is, it is in pain," Arkean said, as he gently pushed his cousin's hand away. "It calls to us for help. I cannot ignore a call for help from man or animal, Bode."

The call for help was overwhelming for Arkean, but Bode was right. They needed to be cautious. They all looked at one another, then reached for their weapons.

Arkean nodded and took the lead. The voice had to be coming from the direction of the opening. It was light out when he found it, and when he looked through the opening then, he saw nothing. Now he could see that a white glow was flickering from somewhere inside the area beyond the opening.

Walking slow and on alert, Arkean went toward the opening. He tried looking through it but the light was too bright he decided to just go inside. It took some effort to squeeze through the opening but each of them made it. They took their combat stances, with Quende and Bode standing with arrows drawn in the rear, just in front of the opening. Arkean and Gedgi crouched with their knives in hand in the front of the party.

It took some time for Arkean's eyes to adjusted to the strange glow illuminating the space. When they did, he saw something move near the far wall. Quende must have seen it to because he jumped back and cursed. Gedgi gasped then fell to his butt, using his heels to push further away. Bode, who was slowly backing away, stumbled into Gedgi but managed to stay on his feet.

Unlike his companions, Arkean didn't recoil from the sight of the thing that cringed in the corner. He heard the pain in its call. He knew from the way it shook that it was badly injured. His instincts never failed him and they were screaming for him to help the creature. So, he paid no attention to his friends' calls and warnings as he slowly approached the large thing that lay a short distance away.

As he got closer, the light that seemed to be coming from the creature began to fade as if it sensed the brightness was hurting Arkean's eyes. When he was close enough to reach out and touch the creature, Arkean gave a sigh of determination and visually examined what was stretched out in front of him.

The creature's body was like a man's, with some noticeable differences. If it stood, the thing would be the height of a man and a half. A dull light surrounded the creature's head but not its grayish blue body. The face was oval with one hole that could have been a mouth, with four slits above it that flapped open every so often like it was used for breathing. The ear-like things coming out of the side of its head were large and pointy and reminded Arkean of the kind of ears you would see on a bat. Its eyes were wide, round, and were oddly the color of the richest blue in the center that appeared light green at the edges.

In the center of its eyes were orange diamond slits that resembled the pupils of a lion. At the end of each leg and hand were three smaller appendages that could be toes and fingers. But the strangest thing to Arkean was that the creature had a large area in the center of its chest where, instead of ribs and organs, sat the biggest crystal stone Arkean had ever laid eyes on. Eight vine-like structures came out of the stone and joined to form four sets of two that went into each "nose" slit.

Arkean was giving the body another once over when the creature moved one of its arms to reach for him. That's when Arkean saw the light-colored liquid running from what appeared to be a large wound under the crystal. Arkean instantly dropped to his knees and covered the gaping wound with his hands as he shouted for Quende, whose father had some knowledge in healing. He was so frantic that he didn't even feel the creature's hand on his.

"There is nothing on this planet that can save me. I am dying, Arkean."

Arkean heard the creature's words clearly and understood them.

"No, we can help you," he said looking over his shoulder to his friends but he was amazed to see only darkness. Darkness surrounded him. His friends and the cave had disappeared and only he and the creature remained.

"It's too late for me. Now listen carefully. I felt your presence, and your spirit is the purest of the four of you so it is you who I will entrust with my legacy. Will you accept my gift?"

Too many questions came to Arkean at that moment. *Gifts...what are you...where did you come from?* But this creature was dying and he would refuse no one their last wish if it was in his power to grant.

Only...

"Where are my friends?"

"They are exactly where they were, where you are. We are still in the cave but I have entered your mind and isolated us so that we won't be distracted. Will you accept my gift?"

Arkean hesitated but the creature must have known because Arkean felt its cold fingers caressing his hands that still lay over its wound.

"There is no reason for you to accept what I offer, but know that I am the last of a gentle race who will no longer taste life. If you accept my gift, a part of us will live on in you. Will you condemn us to total extinction, Arkean?"

Can I deny this creature's plea? Arkean asked himself.

Arkean didn't fully understand the choice at hand but he somehow knew that if he didn't do this, if he didn't accept this "gift" that it would be a mistake that he would regret. Not to mention that everything inside him cried out to protect the creature, to help it.

He felt no malice from the being. He sensed only goodness and truth and yet a fear that no being should ever have to endure was all around it. A feeling of total and utter defeat emanated from its core and into Arkean. This creature was indeed the last of its kind. A warm peace settled inside Arkean and he knew then what he needed to do.

"No, I will not condemn your race to total extinction. What must I do?"

Suddenly, Arkean saw himself standing on a ridge overlooking a vast dark city. Underneath his bare feet, Arkean felt something that resembled grass but it had a mild yellow glow and it was softer. The air around him felt different, thicker, but he had no problem breathing. It was dark all around him but the soft light coming from the grass-like substance gave such a subtle glow that he knew that lighting this place was the purpose of it. In the sky, he saw three large round spheres that resembled the big white thing that floated in the sky above his home at night, but these were colored.

Very little light illuminated the sky…here.

Here…

And just like that, Arkean knew where and what *here* was. He was in the place the creature came from. He was on another…*planet*.

How do I know that?

Then it dawned on Arkean that he knew a lot of other things now. He knew that the big white thing that floated above his home in the sky will be called a moon and that this planet had three but no sun.

"Sun…you have no sun." Arkean looked to the being that stood beside him seemingly whole and uninjured. The being he now knew was called Lette.

Lette looked down at him. "No Arkean, our eyes cannot bear extreme light." Lette extended his hand. Upright, the Ilterian was a giant compared to humans. "This is Ilteria, my home planet."

Arkean smiled at the wonders of the great planet. The plants around him were strange but held a beauty he admired. He inspected them with an appreciative eye that he didn't have for some things on his own planet.

Arkean glanced to his left and a cloud-like image of an Ilterian misted through him. Arkean tensed as the ghost slowly reformed into solid matter as it moved away. In front of him, ghosts of the Ilterians that had once lived here peacefully moved around and through him as they went about their day.

He felt their happiness, their beautiful sparks of life.

Then, a single streak of orange and red fire lit the sky. Arkean looked up and saw several silver vessels streaking across the dark sky. He looked down at the city and its inhabitants as they watched the spectacle in the sky. None of the Ilterians saw the danger. They watched with curiosity as more vessels blazed into their atmosphere. But Arkean knew what was happening. He screamed for them to run, to take shelter, only they couldn't hear him.

It took a moment for him to realize that the attack had already happened and the inhabitants of the planet were already dead. He watched as Lette took several small steps forward. Joining him, Arkean could see the pain and anguish on the Ilterian's face as he watched everything unfold again via his memories. Arkean watched as Lette cringed when the small airships began to fire upon his planet. At this point, the Ilterians seemed to finally understand the severity of the situation. But it was too late.

"Where are your warriors?"

Lette sighed. "My people were a peaceful race. We treasured intelligence and love, not war and anger. We had never experienced or even seen such horrors before."

"You weren't prepared," Arkean whispered.

In a flash, they were no longer standing on the ledge but instead, they were in the city. Amazing tall structures fell all around him, turning into ghost-like clouds before they ghosted through him and hit the ground. Arkean's attention turned to the bodies of the young and old who were littered all around him.

Then, just like he was transported to the city from the ridge, he was suddenly in a spacious building. He saw…*Lette*. It wasn't exactly the Lette that stood beside him now, but Lette in the time of the memory. Arkean knew it was Lette just like he "knew" other things he was seeing. Lette was sitting on the floor and three regally dressed Ilterians were huddled over him, pushing the crystal into his chest. The Lette on the floor let out a scream that drove Arkean to his knees.

"It hurts," Arkean gritted out.

Lette, his guide, placed his three-fingered hand on Arkean's shoulders as he watched his other self-twist and squirm in pain on the floor. "I am sorry my friend. Our connection is stronger than I thought."

With the Ilterian's touch, his pain subsided and Arkean was able to stand again. He'd never felt pain like that before. It felt like something was pulling him apart. He blinked back the tears in his eyes and focused on the scene in front of him.

Lette, the ghost image, was being helped to his feet by the Ilterians who had buried the crystal in his chest.

"Get the crystal to safety Lette, and you must live son." Lette's father and the two others led him to an adjoining room that was a launching station.

"Please dad, you go or send Siet. He is stronger than I am," the ghost Lette begged.

Siet shook his head as they strapped Lette in the ship. "I will not go, my young brother." He grabbed Lette's bat-like ears and pulled him close until their heads touched. "You must live."

"I know you are young Lette, but you can do this. Look inside yourself and find the strength you need." His father cupped Lette's ears and touched their heads in endearment.

Arkean looked up at his guide, Lette. "How old are you?"

"In your culture, I would be ten Sumas or years," Lette said, but his eyes were transfixed on the past version of his kin as the airship he was in began to hover.

Again, Arkean found himself outside. It was chaos as Ilterians ran from translucent corporal creatures with long glimmering horns that adorned narrow faces and wide doe-like eyes. A long gold appendage that was attached to these attractive dreamlike creatures reached out slowly toward the Ilterians they were corralling. Then suddenly the things attacked with the appendages, striking like snakes. Arkean watched as helpless Ilterian after Ilterian shook furiously for several heartbeats only to fall to the glowing grass, motionless.

The same scene was happening all around them.

A loud noise along with screams broke through the destruction, catching Arkean's attention. Lette looked up. Arkean's eyes followed his to see a silver glare streaking across the dark sky. They were in the sky now, hovering over Ilteria.

Lette, who hovered beside him, gave one last look at his home as the life of every living plant, animal, and Ilterian was sucked away. That was when Arkean saw a gigantic pipe extending from a sky vessel that rivaled the planet in size. The pipe had penetrated the planet's surface. The light of the yellow grass dulled as the pipe buried into the planet's surface, deep into its core. The little light of the dark planet flickered several times then died out as Lette's ship sped off into space.

A single enemy ship followed.

"My craft was sucked into a wormhole and I crashed on your planet," Lette told him.

Arkean then found himself standing in the desert he knew so well. He saw Lette's craft half buried in the sand. It was damaged beyond repair.

"I opened the ground up so it swallowed my craft. The attackers of my planet sent one of their own after me and that craft was sucked into the wormhole as well. I couldn't risk it finding me."

The airship began to sink right before Arkean's eyes. He watched the newcomer walk away from his sunken ship to find a new home. They followed the ghost Lette.

"You don't look hurt," Arkean began, "when did you-" Arkean stopped in midsentence.

Four Hyenas came out of nowhere. Their attack was unexpected, swift and deadly. Arkean moved forward to help but it was just a shadow of a memory and when he reached the ghost Lette, a blast of energy rippled through him, throwing the hyenas in the air. One of the hyenas recovered just as ghost Lette got to his feet but the animal was thrown back with such force that it didn't move again. All the others ran off as ghost Lette stumbled forward, clutching his midsection as clear fluid ran through his fingers.

Then, the vision ended.

Arkean was still on his knees, leaning over Lette with his hands pressed over the wound. He looked over his shoulders and realized his friends hadn't moved. They were still in the frightened position they were in when he first touched the Lette.

Just when Arkean thought that his friends weren't going to help, Bode slowly moved toward him.

"What can I do?" his cousin asked with a shaky voice.

Arkean turned to look at Lette. "Can you drink water?"

"What did you just say, Arkean?" Bode gave him a confused look. "What were those words you spoke?"

"I...I asked if he could stomach our water. Why?"

"You spoke my language. As long as we are touching you will be able to understand me and I, you." Lette gurgled. "My body does not need nourishment or sleep the way yours does."

This time when Arkean spoke, he made sure his native tongue was what left his mouth when he looked at Bode. "He needs our help." Arkean reached out with one hand and grabbed Bode's wrist.

Bode twisted back and fell to the ground as he reached for Gedgi with his other hand. Seeing Bode's apparent retreat and fear, Gedgi reach out and grabbed Bode's hand. Quende grabbed Gedgi around the waist, with the intent of pulling them all free.

With his hand firmly around Bode's wrist, Arkean was grateful for the link his cousin and the others unwittingly provided. It would make it easier to transfer the images Lette showed him. Arkean didn't know how he knew it was possible, but he wasn't going to question it. The transfer was instant. What felt like a lifetime passed through them in mere seconds.

Arkean could see the understanding in each of their eyes and knew that they felt the same way he did. He wasn't at all surprised when each of them took a position around Lette, touching the alien.

"*My planet is gone. My people and all our knowledge and our culture will die with me unless we can live in you and your descendants. Do you accept the gift I offer? Will you allow the Ilterian's to live on?*"

Arkean was the first to answer, "I will."

After Lette showed the three what Arkean witnessed through memory, one by one they all agreed. Arkean knew what was required. Lette showed them all how the transference would be done and what would be expected of them as well.

What they were accepting wasn't to be taken lightly but there was no way they could refuse. Arkean could not understand the degree of evil it took for one to invade a place with no purpose but to kill and to destroy, to entirely eradicate a race and their planet. Lette's people didn't deserve what the unknown invaders had done to them. It was unjust and Arkean was honored to help, even though he wasn't sure what the gift entailed and what it would do to him.

When he heard a slight swooshing sound then a click, Arkean looked down at the Crystal in Lette's chest. A reddish-orange fluid began to swirl inside the crystal as the tubing that came from the crystal pulled free of Lette's nose slits. The eight tubes split and merged into four and floated toward Arkean until they were inches away from his chest. Then without warning, all four tubes impaled him.

The initial pain felt like a bee's sting but as liquid pumped from the Crystal into him, it felt like lava. He fell back with his legs still under him as he squirmed. He tried his best to not scream out in agony but the pain was too much. Just as his cry filled the cave, three of the tubes pulled out of him leaving only one.

To their credit, his brethren didn't run when the tubes floated toward each of them. Arkean lay on the floor screaming as he watched the tubes pierce each of them simultaneously. The last thing he remembered was Lette's voice in his head.

"Sleep, strong one."

●

Arkean's body ached and his mouth was dry but other than that he felt fine even though he didn't remember how he ended up where he was. He wasn't at the cave's entrance keeping watch. Then he remembered Lette and everything else came rushing back.

His first thought was for Bode.

Arkean sat up, pushing a wave of dizziness aside. He knew the cave was pitch black but somehow, he could see perfectly through the darkness. Bode must have passed out too because he lay sprawled out beside him. Arkean scooted over to him and shook his shoulder.

"Bode," he said. "Wake up."

Bode grunted. "Please stop shaking me. I feel like I've been run down by an elephant."

Arkean laughed as relief washed over him. He was ashamed that their safety hadn't meant anything to him in the face of Lette's predicament, but his kin seemed fine.

Lette…

Arkean looked over to see Lette's lifeless body. Gedgi and Quende were stirring on the other side of Lette's body. They looked fine so he moved closer to Lette and touched the side of his face where one's cheek would be.

"You hold the bulk of my legacy, Arkean." Arkean heard Lette's voice in his head. One look at his friends told him that they heard the voice too. *"You will be more powerful than the others because of your selflessness and eagerness to aid something as alien as me with no prejudice. Your bloodline with reign and yours alone will bear the Halo, the only one of your kind who will be able to contain all my power.*

"Bode, you are strong and loyal, a king among kings. Your bloodline will infuse your people with strength and determination that will be revered and respected. But it will also breed the Harbinger, the one who will see the answers you all seek but will offer only what you need to know.

"Quende, your bloodline will capture and command that what all Ilterians hold dear. Life, birth and rebirth…change and growth. Nurture the cycle because without it we are all lost.

"And Gedgi, you are the most innocent of the group. You have seen much and still, you have not let the worries of your world or the influences of life's harsh nature wither your soul. It is of that innocence and your spirit that you will bear the essence of Ilteria.

"Each of you must follow your strength from within and support each other. Hold on to this devotion and loyalty I sense between you. Your world is the same but you four have changed. Your bodies and minds will be stronger, you will be

powerful compared to others on this planet but your life can still be taken from injury such as mine has been. Use your intelligence Arkean, your strength Bode, your heart Quende, and your soul Gedgi. You have my thanks and serenity be with you all."

Arkean let his hand fall from Lette's cheek. It was clear that he was in the shade and had been when he gave them his gifts. The voice from his passing soul was nothing more than a whisper. Arkean's eyes traveled over Lette's entire form, his head lowered.

A sense of loss consumed him. It was strong and it held onto him, clawing at the hard-won control he maintained since he was able to understand his parent's death.

"What do we do now?" Gedgi asked. He looked at each of them through wet eyes.

No one said anything for a while. They just sat there dealing with their grief, each in his own way. After several minutes Arkean raised his head. He knew what he needed to do, Lette told him how it was just…he didn't want to.

With a heavy sigh, Arkean stretched his hand toward the Veilex stone and willed it to him. The response was so instantaneous that they were all startled. Arkean even tensed but it was so subtle that no one noticed. He needed to be strong, to show them strength so they would be strong as well.

The clear stone was about the size of a young child's head. It was beveled with smooth edges, and it weighed almost nothing.

"Place your hands on the stone," Arkean told them.

Bode was next to him so he was the first to place his hand on a section of the stone. Quende and Gedgi followed. The stone broke into four even pieces and they each took one.

"We leave now," Arkean said, looking at Lette.

"Shouldn't we bury him?" Quende asked, looking at each of them.

"He gave me instructions," Arkean said.

Gedgi touched Arkean gently on his shoulder and looked at Bode. "We'll pack up and leave you two to it."

As Gedgi and Quende walked away and quietly slipped through the small opening, Bode and Arkean scooted closer to Lette.

"Should we say something?" Bode asked as he placed his hand on Lette's body.

"Peace be with you," Arkean said as he placed his hand on Lette. The body caught fire. It was a pretty blue blaze that engulfed the alien's body, their hands, and their arms. The flame was so intense the body was ash in a matter of seconds but miraculously both Arkean and Bode were uninjured.

Outside the cave, the sun was just rising over the horizon. The four boys stared at the cave from a good distance for several seconds. Then the cave and the surrounding rocks slowly sank into the ground.

They sought out and found the sunken airship and made sure no one would ever find it. When the four began their journey back home, they were wiser, stronger, and wielding the power of the Gods that their great mother used to tell them about.

3

Homecomings

The weather was changing. Eyet never paid much attention to such trivial things as weather or seasons before coming to this place that was so different from her homeland. She'd lived in a palace that was made for Pharaohs. Her meals were prepared for her. Lowly born servants saw to her needs, assisted in dressing her, and painting her face. Life was studies, relaxing, and spending time with her mother and siblings.

Eyet's life changed the day she was chosen by her father to be the mate of a Bodai prince. It was said when she was born that no one had seen a more beautiful baby. As she grew she noticed how people looked at her. Women, some who were to care for her, smiled at her but cut their eyes at her when they thought she wasn't looking. Men watched her with interest. Several requests for her mating was presented to her father before she became suitable for such things.

She was a distraction, her father told her, with his usual impatience on that dreaded day in the great hall. Two of her brothers had been fighting over which would have her. Neither would because her father had been planning since her birth to offer her to the Bodai. He told her that she was a vital pawn in his success; that the Bodai warriors were sent to their kingdom by the god Sekhmet and because of this he had to appease them to ensure their commitment.

Her feelings did not matter, there was nothing she could do. There was nothing anyone could do. To defy her father's pronouncement would mean death, even to her.

So, here she was, inside the Bodai village.

It wasn't what she expected. She imagined twelve-foot-tall, dark-skinned, devil warriors with horns and hooves who would pass her from one bed to another until she was crazed. She was gripped with fear but held her head high when she entered the village two Sumas ago. What she saw was a well-developed community of proud, capable, and dare she admit, handsome men and women.

It wasn't a marble metropolis with temples that reached the clouds, yet it wasn't completely unlivable. The simple dwellings were made like the ones from her home. A large waterfall separated the village into two parts that were connected by three well-crafted small bridges. Trees were incorporated in some of the dwellings and throughout the village.

There were comforts that she enjoyed. She loved the plush bedding that she lay on nightly. There were also times when she was alone with her thoughts, unlike at her home where someone was always following her around. The food was enjoyable and she wasn't constrained by all the frills and decorations that she had to dress in at home.

Eyet soon learned that excess was unnecessary here.

She looked around the space she called home for two Sumas. It was spacious and built to keep the occupants cool and dry. Her space was composed of five single round dwellings that were connected to make one large circle. In the rear of each dwelling was an entryway that let out to a courtyard where there were a small garden and an area where weaving, sewing, gathering, and cooking was usually done. Every single dwelling had spaces inside that was used for things such as dressing and bathing, sleeping, eating, or relaxing when not in the courtyard.

Cire, also an Egyptian princess from Eyet's homeland, was one of the great-mothers and was the elder of the dwelling where Eyet lived. It was decided before Eyet arrived that she would dwell with Cire until Eyet was formally joined with the prince.

Everyone thought that she would more easily learn the ways of the Bodai from one of her own, but Eyet already knew the ways of the Bodai. She was taught from birth, unlike Cire who had to learn when she arrived. But even with knowing their language and some of the customs, Eyet still felt like an outsider.

"One of the sentinels has spotted them," Ivi said breathlessly.

Eyet looked up at Ivi with awe but tried to smother her excitement. Ivi was Bode's younger sister by one Suma. She was tall, slender and attractive, and she lived in one of the dwellings connected to Eyet's. The structure they lived in was inhabited by two others beside Cire, Ivi, and herself.

Mye was a small beautiful girl of eighteen Sumas who was both mute and deaf. She came to the dwelling after Eyet arrived. Eyet didn't know the circumstances surrounding Mye's departure from her family's dwelling, but she did know that Mye was Quende's older sister. The final resident was a young woman who planned to mate one of the most fruitful farmers of the village. She rarely stayed in her dwelling anymore, choosing to stay with his parents until the ceremony.

"You must be ready. Are you ready for the Tandot?" Ivi asked, anxiously moving from one foot to the other.

Eyet saw Mye standing quietly behind Ivi. Her beautiful light brown eyes showed the mixture of worry and excitement her mouth couldn't convey. It was the first time Eyet saw Mye this emotional.

Eyet looked down at her jeweled cup, eyeing it before grabbing it up. "Yes," Eyet said, standing.

At her original home, she and Ivi would walk side by side, being royalty, and Mye would have to follow behind, but Eyet wasn't home and she kind of liked that she wasn't always singled out. She fell in step with the two girls, walking as equals.

It looked as if the entire village had come to the center circle to greet and see the four boys, returning as men, pass by. Eyet saw King Obade with his Queen, Bode's mother, sitting on their ceremonial benches. The King's second mate, Ivi's mother, stood behind the first mate.

Two of Eyet's father's advisors who were there to verify her and Bode's mating was seated beside the King. A small group of the Pharaoh's soldiers was in attendance as well. One of them met her gaze and she quickly turned her attention to the crowd.

Eyet searched the gathering people for Cire. She found the regal older woman sitting on her bench outside the great circle with her belt strings dangling in her hand. Their eyes met and Eyet wished she hadn't sought out the woman because the pain reflected in her gaze was monumental.

"They are saying that only three have returned," a man whispered to another.

Ivi turned around and glared at the man with narrowed eyes. By the way the man looked back at Ivi it was clear he didn't know the princess was near. The man looked away as Ivi's smile faltered and she turned to look at her father.

Eyet knew that Ivi was looking for some telltale sign that would validate or dispel the man's comment, but the King looked worried as well. He would be the first to know which of the four who did not make it. Then he would tell his Queen, then Cire.

Eyet looked to Cire again, now understanding the woman's pain, and a sudden wave of sadness assaulted her. Mye, who must have read the man's words from his lips, scoffed at the man then grabbed Eyet by the hand and tugged her to the center of the circle. Mye let Eyet's hand go when they stood with over three dozen other women who were split into four groups.

Instead of standing with Eyet or joining one of the other groups, Mye moved to the outskirts where Ivi and the rest of the tribe were gathering.

Eyet rolled her shoulders as she stood up straight. She relaxed her face muscles to display interest and nothing more, while inside her heart was splintering. Her legs moved without command until she was standing in the group for Bode, along with approximately eleven other women.

She eyed the other groups, noting the largest. Eyet inwardly grimaced.

But, there were four groups. Taking little comfort in the fact that none of the groups of women were dismissed, Eyet closed her eyes and took a deep breath. When she opened her eyes, she took the time to look the women over. Each was dressed in her best covering as they watched the pathway the four would walk with anticipation. They all had their reasons for entering the Tandot. Some of them were in it for love or the promise of it. Some were here for power, some for appearances, bragging rights, or lust.

Then there was her.

Eyet was a gift. A peace offering that will cement an alliance between her father's people and the Bodai once again.

The crowd watched them, the potentials, with anticipation, wondering which of them will be chosen. If one of the four Warriors who survived the Maatii walked to one of them, sliced his hand, and drained his life's blood into her cup for her to drink, they were officially chosen as a mate. If the male didn't choose a woman it meant he didn't want a mate at that time but could later choose one during any mass gathering. The woman had the right to deny the male by not drinking the Warrior's offering, but to her knowledge, none ever had.

This was the way Guardians chose their mates. The other men in the village had a less public process that just required the male to ask the intended's sire for permission, though most fathers denied those males, holding out for the possibility of a Guardian to claim his daughter during the Tandot.

Eyet found it hard to relax. Her mind raced with worry.

She found Mye in the crowd and used her friend as an anchor. Mye gave her a weak smile. It burned Eyet that the woman wasn't regarded as a proper mate. Mye was one of the most beautiful women in the village but was overlooked because of something she could not control.

Eyet smiled back at Mye before looking over at Cire. The woman was visibly shaking now. Eyet swallowed and silently prayed as she tried to relax.

●

Arkean knew that they should return as a group, they all did. But no one protested when he told them just outside the borders of their lands that he would meet up with them at the main gate.

So much happened while they were away and so many things were different—*he* was different—but at the same time so many things were the same.

Perhaps I am a coward, Arkean thought as walked alone.

It wasn't the change in him that had him stalling. Surprisingly, Arkean and his brethren accepted the changes they were experiencing with ease, not to discount the adjustment phase of wielding such power.

Bode, Gedgi, and Quende were having the time of their lives discovering what they could do. They had the knowledge of their abilities and they instantly knew how to wield a good many of them effortlessly; but for some abilities, they knew they needed skill and practice to effectively use them.

Quende seemed to have the gift to manipulate land, soil, or simply anything that grew. Gedgi could command fire, air, and water. That made crossing the rapids trouble free. Bode seemed to be able to make people do what he willed, though the skill was lost on Arkean and it barely worked on Gedgi and Quende. Arkean found that he had all the abilities the others had and some they didn't.

Arkean moved lazily down the well-used path that led to a grove of trees. The forest was rich in wildlife and most of the animals avoided man, but the Bodai found use of the larger, tamer beasts like the elephants. He moved past the grazing animals slowly. These were wild, and if they felt threatened they could use their large tusks to impale him, or their monstrous feet to stomp him. So, he used caution when he neared them.

One of the animals looked down at him but didn't move. Arkean shrugged and continued toward his purpose. He spotted the purple flowers that Cire loved and quickly picked a bouquet. He regarded the flowers as he walked on the path to home. They were beautiful and he could see why she liked them, but they died too soon for him.

Though, life goes on, doesn't it?

Life went on after his parents died. Life went on for Cire when her mate died. His life would go on too, even without Eyet.

He already decided to accept that Eyet was Bode's, so he just had to show that he meant it by choosing a mate today. There was no reason to prolong the day's proceedings any longer.

The cheers were almost deafening as Arkean slowly moved through and around people to make his way to the center circle. He didn't make it in time to join Bode, Quende, and Gedgi at the stone wall so he entered and followed the moving crowd. Once he was recognized the crowd parted for him until he had a clear path to the center and his Maatii brethren.

Bode, who was kneeling in front of the high thrones, was looking up at his father. "We've all returned," Bode said as Arkean stepped beside him.

There were gasps and cheers but Arkean didn't turn to see why. He kneeled beside Bode, resting the hand that held the flowers on his knee as he lowered his head. Their treasures from the lion kill were laid before their king's feet.

King Obade exhaled then laughed. "I am happy you have returned to us Arkean."

Arkean raised his head and smiled. His uncle loved him like a son and accepted him without pause. "You have given me a home uncle. I will always return."

Arkean turned his head to regard his queen, offering her a smile and that was when he saw them. Dressed in expensive waist linens, neck ornaments, and false hair, the Egyptians looked at him with outward curiosity. He narrowed his eyes and tightened his jaw. His parent's blood was calling out for revenge as he stared into the dark lined eyes of the enemy.

Be still cousin for this is not the time or place." Bode's hand gripped his wrist.

Lowering his head, Arkean shook with anger until the ground vibrated beneath him. A few people must have felt it, because there was some rustling but the ground stopped as he quickly reigned in his emotions. Bode's hand fell away when Arkean relaxed.

The King raised his voice so all could hear. "These four left as boys and have returned as men. Rise warriors, Guardians of Bodai." The four young men rose to their feet. "You are from this day forth the protectors of my people. You will have your own land within my borders. You will eat the best meats, fruits, and enjoy life's comforts. And you may choose a mate if one will have you," he said, then laughed.

The crowd cheered.

Arkean felt Quende brush his shoulder against his.

"What did you promise all of them?" Quende whispered to Arkean.

Arkean looked at Quende who tilted his head to something behind them. He looked over his shoulder at the women who were arranged in four groups. In front of each group of women was a dagger that each boy was told to leave behind. He left the dagger his maternal great father, a Pharaoh who died of natural causes, had given his father Dwar. The dagger was encrusted with jewels and the handle was gold.

"Perhaps the jeweled dagger," Gedgi replied as he stared at Arkean's group in awe. It was clearly the largest.

Arkean frowned at his friends. "I've promised nothing," he told them.

"Take your places," the King urged them.

Bode, Quende, and Gedgi moved forward until each stood in front of his dagger and the group of women.

Arkean moved in unison with them. He tried not to look at Eyet but lost that battle when her white linen gown flared in a light passing breeze. It wasn't smart to look at her, not now, but he was a man in love and he was weak.

Eyet stood proudly facing forward, as radiant as the sun that they all worshiped. Almost as tall as Arkean, she wore her head adornment, though he liked her lovely long black hair flowing freely. Her eyes were lined perfectly; her cheeks naturally blushed in the warm heat. Her lips were full and a soft rose color that promised sweetness while her luminescent tan skin suggested that it was smooth and soft to touch.

Eyet didn't look at him. She never did. So, Arkean turned his attention to the dagger at his feet.

"As Bodai law requires, you have earned your title as Guardians," King Obade said. "You will continue to train and master the skills to be among the best fighters who have ever lived."

King Obade paused to look at Arkean. It was well known that Dwar was one of the best warriors who had ever lived and the King had hopes that Arkean, being his father's child, would be as well.

"You will no longer have to worry yourselves with the duties of the common man because your life is that of a Guardian," the King told them. "A Guardian's duty is to protect his tribe and help our tribe grow. Now choose your first mate to share your life and bear your young."

Arkean bent and picked up his dagger. He rose slower than the others but none of his brethren moved before he straightened. They were to cut their hands with the dagger and drain some blood into the cup of the woman they chose. She would drink, accepting his claim for her. Later, when they were alone, the rest of the marriage ritual would be completed.

After closing his eyes for a moment, Arkean focused on his group. He recognized several of the women but found a girl that he knew well, Loa. She was nice and attractive. Her breasts were full, her hips round. She would bear him nice, healthy young. Arkean took a step forward only to have Bode stretch his arm out to stop him.

"The Tandot must wait," Bode said loud enough for all to hear. He, Quende, and Gedgi placed their ceremonial daggers in their sheaths.

Arkean was confused but he trusted his cousin so he sheathed his dagger as well.

"My King, we have a private matter to discuss with you."

One of the Egyptian advisors stood and began talking so fast that Arkean could barely keep pace with what he said. He said something about a covenant and that Eyet has been with their tribe for too long.

King Obade's response was a slight smile and a few simple words. "Do what you will but know that here…here you are just men not gods. The politics of your people is taxing. And I would like to remind you that the Pharaoh seeks to rebuild the relationship he himself has severed with the murder of one of our warriors who was in the previous Pharaoh's service. I accepted this Pharaoh's peace offering to quell a war between our people. You and your soldiers are my guests…for now…because it seems we each want something from the other. But things can change."

The King then rose to his feet, kissed his Queen's hand and excused himself, before stepping down from his throne. Several Guardians flanked him as he walked to his quarters. The King's two most trusted advisors, Syn, the Ika or medicine man, and Lyar, the Oracle, followed quietly.

Arkean hurried to his great mother Cire and handed her the flowers before he, Bode, and the two others in their group took up the rear behind the advisors. Once in the King's receiving room, Obade told his Guardians to leave them.

Syn and Lyar stood in their usual spot, behind the King's throne to the right. Arkean looked up at them in time to see

Lyar watching him. She was young, voluptuous, and had a sex appeal that seemed to ooze from her pores.

She was also the all-seeing virgin Oracle and was to remain pure according to law. He slightly lowered his head to her, a bow of acknowledgment. Lyar gave him a subtle smile then looked to Bode who was kneeling in front of his father.

"Father, something happened to us on our journey home. We…" Bode glanced back at the rest of his Maatii companions, seemingly looking for help.

Arkean immediately stepped forward and dropped to one knee. "Uncle, we have changed since our last meeting."

"Yes, you are different. You are men now." The King smiled proudly as he looked from Arkean to Bode then back to Arkean. "You will make a fine Guardian Arkean. Just like your father. Stories of your campaigns will be told long after you're gone." King Obade turned to Bode, "And you my son will be a great King."

"It's best if we show you," Bode said, then sighed. He looked at Gedgi who stepped forward with his hands raised, level with his chest.

The air around them began to swirl into a small whirlwind in front of him. Gedgi moved his hand and the swirl of air moved in whatever direction he pointed. Holding the cyclone in place before the King, who was wide-eyed with his mouth gaped open, Gedgi extended his other hand toward the large pitcher of water that sat on a table near the throne. The water came out of the pitcher in a high arc in the air, only to swirl like the air in front of the King.

"Quende," Bode said.

Arkean watched the King to gauge the ruler's reaction. The King was in awe but his expression leaned more toward interest than fear. Syn and Lyar on the other hand, had taken a few steps away from the King's side. Syn looked horrified while Lyar seemed confused.

Quende stepped forward and dug his hand in the soil. He seemed to be searching for something and when he found what he sought, he smiled, flashing his boyish dimples. The earth between his hands began to break apart, making way for a blossoming vine and leaf that grew into a sapling right before their eyes.

Bode moved back, pulling their audience's eyes to him.

"No mind tricks Bode," Arkean whispered in his cousin's mind. *"Look at Syn and Lyar. They may already want to burn us for devilry as it is."*

Bode smiled the said, *"Let them try, cousin."*

Bode pulled anything that wasn't tied down into the air. Eating utensils, seating, papyrus, and ink, it all spun in a wide circle around the four.

Arkean didn't know what he expected but when King Obade looked at him expectantly he almost smiled. At least the King didn't want to burn them at the foot of the throne. Arkean thought of what he could do to show his power. Then it came to him.

He held out his hand with his palm up to show he held nothing in it. Then he walked over to the sapling and Quende moved back to allow him space. Arkean laid his hand on the tree and it instantly ignited in flames.

Heat licked at his skin but he didn't burn. Backing up so his hand moved from the tree, he allowed them to watch it burn for a few seconds, seeing that he held their attention. Then he commanded the fire back to him. The flames narrowed then stretched until the tips of his fingers were ablaze. He pulled the flames slowly into his hand, to show his control.

When Arkean was done, Bode placed all the items he held in the air back in their places. Quende dug his hands in the soil again, retracting the small scorched tree, watching it grow smaller and smaller until it was a leaf then nothing. The ground closed. Gedgi sent the water spiraling through the air and back into the pitcher then let the air go. A gust of wind whipped around them all, blowing everyone but the Four off balance a bit.

King Obade stood. "How…how is this possible?"

"Guards, take these four away for devilry!" Syn yelled.

"No one move," Arkean said as he spun to meet the incoming Guardians. He flipped the first over his shoulder, tossing him in the air to land hard on his back. The next he kicked hard under the knee causing the Guardian to fall forward into a punch to the jaw. Arkean then quickly disabled the remaining six with fast-moving blows and kicks, skillfully outmatching what were previously the best warriors in their tribe.

Arkean looked over his shoulder at Bode, who was giving off strong vibes of anger.

Bode stepped forward, taking up a spear in a fluid motion that didn't falter his stride. "They should die for attacking you. You are a prince," he said through clenched teeth, "You are my blood."

"We must not hurt anyone. Well, not too badly." Arkean smiled, looking over the downed men as they slowly came to. *"They were taking orders."* Still holding the staff of one of the guards, Arkean turned to face the King.

King Obade was watching them with that same pride-filled gaze he had during their demonstration. Arkean knew what they must do. They must show their loyalty.

Arkean moved to stand in front of their King. He spun the staff and handed it to King Obade then dropped to his knees but looked over his shoulder to see what his cousin would do.

Bode clenched his fist tight, breaking the spear in half as he stared at the guards at his feet. He took several deep breaths to calm then he walked over and kneeled beside Arkean. Quende and Gedgi, who both looked just as angry but hadn't moved during the fight, joined them.

The four lowered their heads to their King.

4

New Beginnings

"King Obade," Syn pleaded, "That is no longer your kin. Something has taken them, replaced them with monsters. We must not allow them to li—"

The look King Obade gave Syn was so scathing that the man stumbled back a few steps. It was a good thing he did because the staff Arkean handed the King was now inches away from Syn's throat.

"Finish those words and you will lose you your head." The King narrowed his eyes, "The head that should not even sit upon your body right now for giving orders in my place." The King allowed the staff to slide to the floor but kept it in his hand as his gaze fell back to the four boys who were still kneeling. "Something has taken them. They are not themselves," he said to himself. King Obade then raised his head. "Bode, what did I tell you, and only you, before you set out for the Maatii?"

Bode looked up but didn't speak. Arkean knew his cousin well enough to know he was embarrassed.

"Tell me, son," King Obade demanded as he arched his brow.

Bode looked at him then away so fast that he didn't think the King noticed. "You said that tonight will be the night that I will really become a man. That when I lay with my mate it will be one of the most pleasurable experiences I will ever have."

The King smiled and patted Bode on the shoulder. "Arkean," he then said, "What does your great mother call you when no one is around?"

"Amun's gift," Arkean answered instantly.

His uncle laughed loud and hard. "That, you may just be. It seems to me that the boys are themselves and more. Lyar, what do you think?"

Lyar's beautiful eyes fell on them, lingering on Arkean.

Arkean wondered why she hadn't spoken yet. Lyar was outspoken and confident. She always had an opinion.

She swallowed then smiled. "I think we have four Guardians who will be unmatched in battle my King."

"Leave us Syn," the King said as he motioned for them to rise. He pulled Bode and Arkean into him for a hug.

"But…my King," Syn begged.

"Would you like to discuss it further, Syn?" King Obade hissed.

Everyone recognized an out when the King was giving it. Apparently Syn knew too because he hastily retreated.

"Come," King Obade told them, "Let us share with our people the gifts our great mother's Gods have given you four."

●

Arkean pushed the fabric under water and started scrubbing the ends together. He repeated this several times before pulling the fabric out and looking it over. He dunked the item underwater again.

"Washing isn't how you should be spending your time, Guardian. Fun is what you should be having when you aren't training," Cire said.

As a warrior, that is all you are. The warrior's job is to protect the village, but Arkean loved learning how to do other things. He enjoyed fishing, weaving baskets, working with metal, even cooking. So, on his day of rest, Arkean chose to do what he usually did on rest days before the Maatii, helping others with their work and learning different trades. This day, Arkean was scrubbing coverings and fabrics with his great mother.

Arkean looked over at Cire. "I find this soothing," he said as he looked back down at his hands and continued scrubbing.

"I see the way you look at her."

Arkean stiffened but didn't raise his head to look across the field at Eyet or back at Cire. He almost pulled his hands free of the water but managed to show no visible reaction.

"Don't look so stricken, Arkean." Her gentle hand brushed his under the water.

He looked over at the only mother he'd known. Her beautiful skin had a light sand tint to it that hid her lifetime well. Her long dark hair was plaited and hung below her waist. She offered him a worried smile when he didn't relax.

"I would never do anything to hurt Bode," Arkean said under his breath. Arkean shamefully kept his head down.

"Arkean, I am not accusing you of trying to hurt your kin. I am simply saying that I…see," Cire said.

Of course, if anyone knew how he felt about Eyet, it was Cire.

When Eyet first came to them, she stayed in her quarters and rarely talked to anyone other than Cire. It was Cire who came to him and asked that he come by when Eyet had sunk into herself, shutting everyone out.

Arkean remembered that day like he remembered every day he was near her. He stepped into the common area and saw Eyet weaving a small basket. It was something she learned in the twelve days she'd been with them. That day, Eyet looked him directly in the eyes.

Arkean looked over at Eyet. At the same time, she looked up and their eyes met and he was instantly transported to the day she arrived in their village looking like a living goddess. Her hair was covered with a braided wig that came just under her delicate jawline. Her eyes, a soft light brown that was lined with black, looked him over as if he were a slave who needed her approval.

Even after Eyet examined him that day, she did not shy away like most girls did. She held his gaze until he kneeled before her and lowered his head in respect of her title as a princess. In her language, Arkean told her his name but she just stared at him as he sat next to her and began weaving.

Arkean learned to weave even though it wasn't something the men did but he liked to visit with Cire, and weaving was usually what she did during his visits. Arkean and Eyet sat most of that day in silence, both weaving and deep in thought. When he placed his unfinished basket in his usual corner and stood to leave, he turned to tell her goodbye but was surprised to see that she was standing in front of him.

"Thank you for being kind to me," she'd told him. And before he could respond, Eyet wrapped her arms around his waist and hugged him tight.

Eyet seemed so leery of him the entire time yet she held onto to him like he was all that stood between her and death. He was younger then. Eyet was younger too but that day he knew that he would never treasure another's touch like he did hers at that moment.

His mind now firmly in the present, Arkean focused on his chore and tried not to look away from Eyet who was walking his way with that beautiful but friendly smile of hers. That friendship smile was all she gave him, all she could and would ever give and that fact speared him right through the heart.

He stood and waited for Cire to stand. Arkean placed his hand gently on great mother's cheek and said, "I will not be back." He pulled her into his arms and hugged her.

"Arkean—" Cire began.

"No," he said, then he pulled away and touched her cheek. "If you know, then think of how many others who may know as well. I have a feeling that Bode does." He moved around her and headed through her dwelling before Eyet could join them.

He heard Eyet ask Cire where he was headed. Cire's reply was simple. She told Eyet that he had come to say that he had outgrown woman's work.

Arkean headed straight for his dwelling on the outer side of the village, near the far western wall. The Guardian's dwellings were placed around the inside borders of the village to make it easier for them to defend the people of their tribe who were housed near the center of the village. The King's dwelling was also near the center.

As he walked, Arkean couldn't help but wonder why Bode hadn't claimed Eyet yet. She was so beautiful that even the King was tempted to add her to his harem, yet Bode delayed. Sixty days had passed since the failed Tandot and the revealing of what they were now capable.

Yet, Bode still waited.

Why? Arkean asked himself as he passed an old man, one of the tribe's fishermen. The man moved out of his way, giving him a wide berth.

As Arkean continued to his dwelling, he looked around. A great number of the villagers waved and spoke when he made eye contact. He spoke to those who spoke to him with as much cheer as he could muster. But a small number just eyed him suspiciously. He could feel their fear as if it was a covering around his body.

He knew not everyone would embrace the change in him and his brethren. He would admit that he was shocked that his uncle, the King, had accepted them so easily. But he had. If nothing more, the King must have deduced the advantage that having four Guardians with special abilities would provide.

Yet, some were frightened by them and what they could do. Some of them were vocal about their concerns, like Syn. Others just kept their distance.

How does Eyet feel? he wondered.

She was raised with irrational beliefs. Her people had many Gods and Goddesses that were praised for their good and feared for their evil. Did she think the four of them were omens?

No.

Eyet was there during the King's presentation of them. With her own eyes, she saw them do the same acts they did for the King. She remained calm through it all even as people around her gasped with surprise or whispered warnings.

Even when one of the Egyptian emissaries tried to pull her away, saying that she was to return to Memphis, Eyet refused. She didn't flinch at Bode's touch when he pulled her from the Egyptian's grasp and pushed the man several feet away with only a flick of his wrist. Instead, Eyet locked her arms around Bode's waist and buried her head in his chest. Arkean, Quende, and Gedgi stood beside their prince and his intended mate, against the Egyptians.

The image of Eyet and Bode holding one another caused him pause, and saved the Egyptians that day.

Arkean placed his hand over his aching chest. How was he going to live with the Bodai after Bode and Eyet completed their union? Knowing that Bode would touch her in the places he wanted to so desperately, almost dropped him to his knees. He would have to endure trials and heartache that would drive a lesser man mad. He had to harden his heart for Eyet and protect Bode with his life.

He had no choice.

"Are you ok?" Hetu asked him as she tugged on his kilt. She smiled at him when he looked down at her.

Arkean bent to lift her up in his arms. Hetu was Gedgi's little sister and a precious gift to their tribe. All the Bodai women were precious to them and treasured because there were so few. There were about ten Bodai males per every Bodai female. A sickness that only affected the women had swept through their numbers long ago. No witchdoctor, prayers, or remedies worked to increase the number of females born.

It is why the Bodai Kings of old treasured the agreement of ten Bodai warriors for one Egyptian princess. The Bodai tribe gained another woman who could breed. It was believed that the princesses were free of the ailment that caused the

Bodai women to breed mostly male offspring. Overall, the Egyptian princesses did birth more females.

"I'm fine Hetu," Arkean said as he kissed her on her head. She was a pretty girl but often ran around with the boys, doing boy things. "How are you?"

"I well," she grinned. "You mate yet?" It was the same question she asked him since the failed Tandot.

"No, my little Hetu, I have not." Arkean carried Hetu toward her dwelling where he saw her mother, Gedgi, and Quende. His friends were repairing the roof using their abilities. They seemed to not care what anyone thought about it.

Hetu's grin widened. "You mate Hetu then."

Arkean laughed.

"Ahh," Gedgi's mother said. She smiled and nodded her thanks to Arkean as she extended her arms to take her daughter. "Come small one," the woman said when Hetu ignored her gesture by locking her arms around his neck.

"I want to go fishing with Arkean," Hetu said.

Arkean cursed to himself. He forgot that he promised his friends that they would go fishing on their break day.

"Hey Arkean," Gedgi called from on top of the roof. "I don't think we'll be done with this and the rest of the repairs today. Maybe we can go fishing next break day."

As he handed Hetu to her mother against the child's best efforts to stay attached to his neck, he looked up and said, "Sounds good. Do you need any help?"

"No," Quende called down, "we have it under control. Just tell Bode that we are busy. I think he is already there."

"I will let him know." Arkean patted Hetu on the head then nodded to her mother before starting off to his dwelling again. He had to get his head straight first before seeing his cousin.

Stepping inside his private dwelling, Arkean tried to release all the tension from his body. He tied a dark cloth to the opening of his dwelling, a signal to anyone who came calling that he was not up for company. He headed to his bedchamber where he immediately lay on his thick bedding and closed out everything—every noise, every thought—and tried to relax.

His peace lasted only five minutes. He sensed her presence almost immediately.

"I do not wish to be disturbed, Lyar." He didn't need to open his eyes to know that she was standing in the doorway of his bedchambers.

"I only wish to give you what I think you may need."

Her husky voice was breathier than he recalled. "What is that?"

"Me," she said.

Arkean heard the distinct sound of fabric falling to the floor. He opened his eyes as he sat up on one elbow. Standing in his doorway was a gloriously naked Oracle. Lyar's hair was mounted atop her head like a crown. His eyes traced luscious curves and womanly mounds as she moved toward his bedding and him. Arkean sat up at the exact moment her large full breasts were directly in front of his eyes. Unable to help himself, he let his gaze lower to the curly mass that covered her core.

"I've waited patiently for the opportunity to have you. And now here we are," she touched his face.

Her touch was nice but didn't warm him like Eyet's. And that was the problem.

Arkean knew he had to stop comparing every female to Eyet, especially at times like this.

Confused, Arkean spoke. "I am pleased that you think of me a worthy male but you are untouched, Oracle. No man is to have you or the Sight will leave you."

"I know you don't believe that, Arkean. You are smart, I know this. My birth wasn't a miracle. My mother lay with so many of our men that there is no way to know who fathered me. And as for the Sight, it is superstition—merely a tradition that allowed the Kings of old to have another beautiful female of the village in their bedchambers when they had mated their limit." She took his hand in hers and placed it on her breast.

She flexed her hand, causing him to squeeze.

The soft, warm, feeling beneath his hand felt…nice, and Lyar's moan was so tempting that he closed his eyes.

He knew that Seer was just a title but had no intention of telling anyone his thoughts on the matter. If the Kings decided to take the opinions of someone, regardless the reason, it was their business. And to be honest, Lyar's mother had been a good, capable advisor. Lyar was too, at times, but Arkean felt that the decisions she made always benefited her in the end.

Arkean slid his hand from her tempting flesh and stood. She backed up a few steps to give him room. He paid attention to her hips as she moved in a way that caused his groin to throb. Lyar was good at seduction but he was beyond the wiles of women.

He had never fallen for a woman's tempting games and he wouldn't ever. A Guardian was to be strong in will and their seed was for their mates. No self-respecting warrior would risk giving his offspring to anyone other than his mates.

"I cannot give you what you want Lyar. You know that I can only offer my seed to my mate."

Lyar smiled. It would have been sexy on another but on her, it was somehow disturbing.

"I saw you at the Tandot those many days ago. None of those females held your interest. I suspect you were going to choose the one whose name you recalled first."

Arkean frowned. She was close but he would never admit it. "It doesn't matter what you think, Lyar. You are the Seer and I am a Guardian. You can no more be mine as I can be yours."

"Oh, I *can* be yours." Lyar moved into him, pressing her full breasts against his chest.

She was so beautiful and alluring that Arkean placed both his hands on her hips and pulled her closer before gently pushing her away.

"I know you want me. I have saved myself for you and you alone. I vow to take no other to my bed if you will have me." Lyar looked up at him as she spoke her vow.

He could do worse than to have one of the most desirable women as his mate. Maybe this was what he needed to forget his fixation with Eyet. He leaned in close to her ear and asked her, "Would you be a Guardian's mate, Lyar?"

Her body tensed and her eyes faltered. She took a few steps back. Her full lips seemed to be searching for the right words as they opened and closed several times.

"I see," Arkean said with a smile. "You will take my seed but will never allow me to claim you or any child you bear as my own."

"You must understand Arkean. My name and title I carry are all I have. To throw that away for—"

"For me," he said, cutting her off. Arkean moved around her and picked up her covering and held it out for her to take. When she didn't take it, he looked back at her. Lyar seemed as if she was fighting a struggle within herself. "If I must couple without love then I will have the title of father to my own child. It is my right."

"You have my heart Arkean," Lyar sputtered out. "You've always had it and I want to give you my flesh but my position as Seer is important to me. I thought you of all people would understand that."

"I do," Arkean said holding her covering up higher.

Lyar took her covering and pulled it over her head. "We could have been good together Arkean."

"I want a mate who will be proud that I have claimed her and who will happily bear me young I can claim."

He watched as Lyar frowned at his words. When he said no more, she raised her head high and composed herself. She transformed from sultry vixen to angry female in no time at all. Her hands flexed into fists and her eyes narrowed when she looked back up at him.

"You should not turn me away, Arkean," she hissed.

Arkean shrugged with indifference. He might regret not bedding Lyar, what male wouldn't? But he would never regret wanting a woman for himself and the children she will bear him to cherish.

He watched her square her shoulders, look through his entrance to make sure no one saw her leaving, then left with her head held high.

Arkean frowned. That whole conversation drained him. For the first time in ninety sunsets he was exhausted. Not because of the training. He could train for days, weeks without rest. His body rarely tired, though his mind…that was another matter.

Everything led back to her. Eyet was consuming all his thoughts. If he was hungry, he wondered if she was eating properly. The weather had him wondering how she was dressed and if she was comfortable. During training, he trained harder so that he would be able to protect her from any attack. When he bathed…his thoughts of her…were private.

Arkean thought about how the Pharaoh would respond to Bode refusing to allow Eyet to return to Memphis.

Did Bode refuse to let Eyet go because of the love he has for her?

5

A Quiet Heart

Sunlight glistened over the moving water as it flowed downstream. The sounds made by moving waters were soothing. It was something Bode never took the time to appreciate. There were so many things he was beginning to take notice of that he didn't appreciate before Lette's gifts.

Like, how beautiful the simple flow of nature was or how just a smile from someone could positively affect his day.

Bode leaned back on the rock and laughed while he watched Mye dance around in the water as fish brushed against her legs. She held her bunched up covering in her hands as she waded through the knee-deep water with high steps as if doing so would help prevent the fish from brushing across her exposed skin.

Mye's smile and silent laugh were so lovely that they were contagious.

His movement must have alerted her because she looked up and her gaze fell on him. Mye stopped moving and laughing, then looked down into the clear water as if embarrassed.

Bode fell silent when she shot him a confused frown. But he continued to watch her move toward the shore. He bit back another burst of laughter when she slipped. To catch her balance, Mye dropped her covering to use her arms to balance herself. Her face scrunched up and she slammed her fist into the water, creating a large splash that wet her upper body.

"Need some help?" Bode asked, using hand signal and trying not to smile.

Mye quickly slashed her hand out in front of her.

It was her way of saying no and it was one of many things he now found utterly charming about her. Ok, maybe he had always known how beautiful Mye was but generally, his mind wasn't on women. It was on being a Guardian and a good future king.

Besides, his queen had already been chosen for him. However, ever since coming back from the Maatii, not only did Bode notice things that made the world beautiful, he also began to think of what he wanted and not what others wanted for him.

Since his return, many things were clearer.

Such as the number of people who were involved in directing the course of his life. If he learned one thing from his experience with Lette, it was that life was short and it was imperative that one should be as happy as they can be; which is why he was out here soaking up the rays and listening to nature's sweet song.

Why Mye was out here alone, away from their village was a mystery though.

So, when she climbed out of the water, stomped toward him, scaled the large stone, and stood over him, he asked. Not in the usual way he communicated with Mye but with a subtle whisper in her mind.

"Why are you here without a companion or Quende?"

Mye jumped back. The irritation that radiated from her gentle soul faded as her eyes widened with surprise.

Bode stretched his hand out to her. *"Please, I didn't mean to scare you. It's just that we may understand each other better this way."*

Slowly, Mye visibly relaxed as she stared at him.

"We can go back to the other way Mye, if you like it better."

Mye seemed to think it over for a moment then shook her head, still in disbelief.

Bode smiled. *"Just think of what you want to say to me and I will hear it."*

Mye raised her brows and thought, *"Can you read my mind, Bode?"*

Bode closed his eyes and settled back against the rock as he let the mental sound of her voice flow through him. Her tone was unsure but it was sweet and soft, like the sound of the wind.

"Bode…can you hear me. Am I doing it right?"

He took several more seconds to enjoy the soft touch of her inner voice before he responded. *"I hear you, Mye. And yes, I can read your mind…but I won't. What we are doing now is communicating by will. You wanted me to hear you so I can."*

She thought over that as well then nodded.

With her trust, he decided to return to his previous question. *"Why are you out alone?"*

"I," she began then stood straighter and lifted her chin. *"I am no child Bode, son of Obade. I may come and go as I please."*

Really? Bode grinned inside but put on his most serious expression and raised a brow. *"Is that right?"*

Mye's eyes widened again. *"No, Bode,"* she said, dropping to one knee, *"I did not mean to-"*

Bode jumped to his feet and placed his hands on Mye's bare arms. He resisted the urge to run his hands up over her shoulders, to feel her soft skin.

He was usually never…curious when regarding a female.

Bode had one of the most beautiful women in the world waiting for his claim, but Eyet didn't make him laugh. She didn't peak his curiosity. She didn't make him feel. If he were to be completely honest, Eyet had no effect on him at all. All he felt for her was an intense friendship and nothing more.

However, since his return from the Maatii, he stirred for Mye. But what man who laid eyes on her could deny the pull of her curves and lovely visage? Even her father…

Just the thought of the man touching *his* Mye burned Bode deep inside.

"I am sorry," she winced.

Bode quickly let go of Mye's arms, paling at the finger imprints he left on her skin. "Gods, I'm sorry Mye. I don't…I didn't mean to hurt you," he stuttered aloud. Then he transferred the thought to her.

Her brows creased and she gave him a wary look.

Did I hurt her much? He needed to be careful with her.

"*You did not.*"

There it was again. Her voice caressed him and his body reacted.

Bode tried to act as normal as possible while he watched Mye's eyes move over his face for a moment. It was as if she was seeing something in him for the first time.

Whatever it was must have scared her because she took a step back. She must have forgotten that her dress dripped water and that where she stood on the smooth rock was now a puddle. Her foot slipped on the slick rock and she fell back with arms flailing for purchase.

Bode reacted swiftly by wrapping his arm around Mye's waist and pulling her into him. He felt a mixture of wet cool cloth and soft female against his skin. He focused on Mye's eyes then his gaze fell to her parted lips.

My Mye? *Do I think of her as mine*? he asked himself.

Bode felt a surge of protectiveness rise in him. "*You must not travel alone, Mye,*" he transferred.

Mye frowned, "*Can I not trust you, Bode?*" Her eyes searched his.

Bode closed his eyes for a moment as he dismissed how badly he wanted to touch his lips to hers. He straightened, making sure she was stable in his arms, then jumped several feet to the ground with her secured. They landed softly and he reluctantly let her go then moved away. When he finally opened his eyes, he transferred, "*I want to do many things to you Mye, but hurting you, I could never do.*"

Mye's face lit up with a smile he never saw before.

Bode didn't expect what happened next. If he had read her mind maybe he would have been prepared for when she stretched upward, leaned into him, then touched her lips to his.

●

A constant thudding pulled Arkean from the haze of sleep. He blinked several times then rolled to a seated position on his bedding. He glanced at Bode as he rubbed his head.

"Am I late for evening feast?"

Bode relaxed against the wall. He chuckled. "It's midday, cousin. You've been asleep for a while but it is not yet evening. Did you rest well?"

"I did." Arkean noticed that his voice sounded a bit deeper.

"Good," Bode said, pushing off the wall. "Dress for battle."

Arkean lifted his head. He looked over Bode for the first time since waking. His cousin had his bow slung over his chest, arrows sheaved in their leather bag, and knives strapped to his thighs and arms. Thick, wide leather bracelets ran from Bode's wrist to his elbows while a leather vest covered his chest. The only thing that separated Bode's war garb from the other Guardians' was the gold, ruby, diamond, and emerald choker around his neck.

"Who is the aggressor?" Getting to his feet, Arkean went to the fresh water bowl that the women refreshed throughout the day and splashed his face and neck.

"The Pharaoh has sent his advisors with demands."

Bode's flat tone spoke volumes. Arkean sensed that Bode was not concerned about the threat the great nation posed.

Arkean stiffened but tried hard to relax, not wanting his cousin to see him as weak. It wasn't war that he feared. He feared losing the one woman he didn't have. What would he do if she decided to leave with the Pharaoh's advisors?

Bode lay his hand on Arkean's shoulder and squeezed. "I will wait outside while you get ready."

Arkean silently cursed. He didn't even hear Bode move toward him even though he could hear people talking in hushed voices three dwellings away. That was unacceptable. He needed to concentrate or he was going to get himself or one of the others killed.

Splashing water over his face again, Arkean cleared his thoughts and focused on the possible battle ahead. He quickly dressed in the same war garbs Bode wore, except around his neck was a band of gold with one diamond that signified his place in the royal family.

With his mind on the threat, Arkean walked beside his cousin to the center of the village. During wartime, their most precious possessions, the women and children, were moved to an underground bunker while the Guardians did what was needed to ensure their protection.

When they arrived at King Obade's dwelling, Guardians were posted outside and inside. Quende and Gedgi waited outside for orders, along with four other Guardians.

Inside, Syn and Lyar stood quietly behind the King. Who Arkean didn't expect to see was Eyet, who stood beside the Guardian Commander. Arkean looked at Bode for answers but Bode shrugged. Arkean and Bode looked at the King, both reading his intentions.

Bode frowned with understanding. *"He plans to harm her if the Pharaoh's men don't back off,"* Bode transferred to Arkean. *"I won't let that happen."*

Arkean could only imagine what motivated his cousin, but he was grateful because he had no right to interfere.

Bode bowed to his King and father then stood straight and extended a hand to Eyet. "Why are you not hidden away with the other women, Eyet? I would not see you injured in any way."

Eyet looked at the King then to the Guardian commander before slowly moving to take Bode's outstretched hand.

Arkean saw a shimmer of fear in her eyes and it angered him that she had reason to be afraid, but he kept his expression calm.

"Quende, Gedgi, please see that Eyet is tucked away safely with my great-mother, where she belongs during times of unrest," Bode said. Or rather ordered. His tone offered no option for refusal.

Arkean managed to keep his eyes forward and did not look at Eyet as she passed.

"King Obade," Syn said as he stepped from behind the throne, "if we give the princess back we can avoid conflict."

Bode sneered at Syn. "I won't have her returned."

King Obade smiled at his son. "Eyet is Bode's intended and her care is his responsibility." The King looked to the Commander and asked, "Are we ready for an attack?"

The Commander stepped forward and bowed. "My King, we are prepared for an attack. The Pharaoh's forces outnumber ours but we are stronger and better trained. We may be able to hold them off long enough to send for our allies."

"We will be destroyed if we do not give back the princess," Syn said with irritation.

"It is something to consider my King," the Commander added.

The King looked at Arkean. It was discussed among the elders that Arkean would be the one to take over as Commander of the Guardians when he had more experience. His father was a great commander and the Bodai believed that such knowledge and skill carried on in the blood.

"What would you do?" the King asked Arkean.

Arkean stepped forward and bowed his head. "I would send me, Uncle…alone."

Bode shook his head as he stepped forward. "You go nowhere alone."

"We go as a team," Quende said as he and Gedgi walked back inside.

The king nodded. "Then, the four will engage first," King Obade said. "Arkean will speak for me today. Commander, you will go to assist."

Syn, the King's adviser, shook his head as he and the Commander spoke at the same time. "My King—"

King Obade raised his hand, "It is decided." The King's gaze bore into Arkean, "Keep my son and yourself safe, son of my brother."

Arkean nodded then he and his entourage left for the main gate.

Arkean felt no presence of the enemy until he and the small band of Guardians crossed Bodai border, beyond the trees. A small group of the Pharaoh's males stood waiting but he sensed a hiding multitude nearby.

Stopping close enough that the Egyptians could see them, the Bodai waited. When two Egyptians started for them, Arkean mentally told the others to stay put while he and the Commander moved forward.

A hundred feet from the Egyptians, the Commander grunted as he reached for his blade. Arkean's vision was more acute than the Commander's so he knew it was a scroll that one of the Egyptian's carried and not a weapon. He placed his hand on the Commander's arm before he could pull a knife in defense.

The Commander gave Arkean an irritated look before moving his hand away from the knife handle. Arkean knew the man was angry. The Commander had been in charge for several Sumas; he worried about his position. But he had nothing to worry over. Arkean just wanted to help his tribesmen, not steal their positions.

Arkean looked at the males who approached. He had an idea of why the Egyptians were here, all four hundred of them. When Arkean and his three brethren returned from their Maatii, he looked into the advisor's mind. He knew the Advisor would tell the Pharaoh what he witnessed. Yes, the

Pharaoh was angry that his daughter had not been claimed yet, but it was something else the Pharaoh coveted.

"Bodai Warrior," the Egyptian said when they were mere feet away. His face was free of hair, giving him a younger look. His wrap was made of fine linen and he wore a braided wig and jewelry. He was the exact opposite of the soldier who stood beside him. "And Royal," the advisor said as he bowed his head to Arkean. "My Pharaoh has been slighted and to avoid war between our people, he would like these demands met."

Arkean looked at the scroll but didn't reach for it. He raised his gaze to the carrier, the advisor. After several tense seconds, the Commander reached for the scroll. Before the Commander finished reading the demands, Arkean said flatly, "Tell your legion that we are prepared for war. But hear me well, Advisor, when I tell you that none of you will survive. You were there to witness me and my brethren's acts, you know we are changed. I am definite that is why your Pharaoh demands that we allow you to shackle and return us four to him." This Advisor was the same Egyptian who tried to take Eyet at their homecoming. Arkean smiled then said, "Your Pharaoh's demands will not be met."

The Advisor and the soldier looked confused for a moment, then what Arkean said to them finally sank in. The soldier's eyes moved over Arkean, probably thinking about how young and inexperienced he looked.

"This is not a game boy. You will die if you continue on this course," the soldier said, with a grave expression on his face.

"I am Arkean, son of Dwar. I have never enjoyed games." There it was—fear. Arkean sensed it from the Egyptians almost immediately after mentioning his father's name. "Prepare yourselves," he said to the Egyptians in their tongue. Arkean then looked at his Commander. "We are finished here."

For a moment the Commander was hesitant to leave, either because he didn't like being ordered or the fact that he didn't finish reading the terms, but Arkean spoke for the King and that meant his words were to be followed.

The Commander lifted his chin, handed the scroll back, then spun around and moved toward their side of the field. Arkean followed, turning his back on their audience.

Later, after checking on Cire and the other women and children, Arkean sat beside King Obade during evening feast. He felt Lyar's eyes on him several times during the meal but he didn't once look her way.

The Commander sat on the other side of Arkean. He followed the conversation about strategy; every so often adding or disagreeing with something said.

"Arkean," The King said as he lifted his cup to his lips, "how would you handle this threat?"

Arkean swallowed the meat he was chewing and wiped his mouth before answering. "The Pharaoh wants Guardians because he knows how skilled we are. He knows of Bode, Gedgi, Quende, and myself and he now wants us too. The Egyptians expect us to cower because their combined forces outnumber us 100 to 1, yet they only sent a small force to accompany their demands. He doesn't believe we will make a stand."

"We cannot fight such forces," Syn broke in, ignoring Arkean. He sat next to Bode, his face pinched in a frown as he listened to the conversation. "We must make an agreement. Give him two who carry the demons." Syn turned to look at Quende and Gedgi then back to the King. "Let the demons curse their village, not ours."

Arkean looked to Gedgi and Quende. Neither seemed fazed by the witchdoctor's remark. "The Pharaoh may be appeased for a time but he will not settle until he gets what he is set on," Arkean said.

The King seemed to consider what both he and Syn said, then spoke, "I will not willingly offer our newfound strength to the bloodthirsty Pharaoh."

"Then we go to war," Bode shrugged from his position on the other side of the King.

Syn immediately stood. He said nothing as he left.

The rest of the meal was spent planning a defense. Arkean suggested that the King send him and him alone to the frontlines. But Bode, Quende, and Gedgi would not hear of it. Bode suggested another plan—that the four confront the Egyptians with only two dozen Guardians as backup.

King Obade didn't seem to like the fact that his eldest son and the son of his brother were going to be on the front lines with such a small group but he seemed to believe the Sun favored them and would not deny the brethren their first battle.

Once plans were set in place, Arkean excused himself and went to his dwelling. His thought as he lay on his bedding, was that he may not have the Pharaoh in his clutches just yet but he was getting closer. Revenge lay just beneath the surface of his thoughts, but he had never expressed his plans to another living soul. Now he was about to get his chance to avenge his parents. Yet he couldn't help wondering what his revenge would cost.

6

Syn moved out of the shadows of the trees to stand before the Oracle. He watched her for a few minutes as she stood impatiently waiting for him to arrive. She was young, beautiful, and apparently, she was immune to his charms. Charms that he used to bed some of his followers who were mated to others. His charms gained him extra nourishment and supplies that he would otherwise have to work for.

"What do you want, Syn?" Lyar asked.

"To discuss the changes in the King and the beast who now walk among us." He watched her closely to gauge her reaction. As a Seer, Lyar was quite the little actress.

"Be careful medicine man," she said, raising a brow.

Syn relaxed back against the tree. He knew that Lyar disliked the Four, the name the beasts were being called, and the new shift in power more than he did. "I was there when Quende and Gedgi made you look like a fool. I know you grow tired of them."

It was during a gathering a few days past that Lyar went into her trance and spoke with the knowing tongue of the ancients. She informed the people that no plant, fruit, or weed would ever grow on any land tended by a young female called Loa. Crops the land provided were important to the Bodai and to say that a female's touch was barren meant no man would risk mating her.

Lyar was smart and cunning like her mother before her. Syn knew her well and kept a close eye on her dealings. Before Lyar made any predictions, she prepared. She read the signs, animal behavior, and even relied on gossip to maintain her stellar reputation. Lyar even went to the depths of concocting some brew to poison Loa's garden to prove her word was bond. What the beauty didn't count on was those devils,

Quende and Gedgi, to make her look like a deceiver. With a touch from Quende, Loa's garden grew like no others.

"Loa is nothing," Lyar hissed.

Syn had even been fouled up by the devils. So many times, in fact, that the tribe's people were beginning to turn to them for aid instead of him, the tribe's medicine man. His supplies were quickly dwindling now that the people were offering his fees to the devils. And to think, the two fools refused to even accept the payments. He knew no good would come from the devils being allowed to live. Now he had to get rid of them before he not only lost his cushy position at the King's side but before he starved.

Syn focused on Lyar. He wondered what he looked like to her. His eyes were probably glossed over and he may even look a little crazy so he focused on her lips and pretended that he was just watching her.

Syn laughed, thinking she should be used to his attention. He didn't want her to know just how much those devils affected him. He wanted her to believe that his proposed scheme was not just self-serving but beneficial to them both.

Lyar narrowed her eyes and balled up her fist. "And for them to help her…" Her words faded then were followed with an angry grunt. She nervously looked away when he frowned at her anger.

Why that reaction? What am I missing?

"You are angry because Arkean was going to choose, Loa," Syn accused, but it was just a spoken thought. When he saw the brief flare of confirmation in Lyar's eyes, he laughed heartily, causing his belly to bounce up and down.

Of course, Lyar had her eyes on the Guardian. Syn should have seen it earlier. The way she watched Arkean, agreed with everything he said and did. It made perfect sense.

"That is why you will not share my bed," Syn added.

Lyar snorted a laugh. "I will not share your bed because you are a man who enjoys the fruits of everyone else's labors. You lay around with the women when you could have been a

Guardian, instead of a round belly man waiting for someone to bring him his next meal. You are arrogant, greedy, and your beady little eyes are always on my breast or bottom like some kind of animal in heat."

Syn grabbed her arm, digging his nails into her flesh. "Do not think you are better than I, Lyar. You are the offspring of the village whore who knew not which tribesman's seed it took to create you. Yes, you are beautiful," he admitted, pulling her closer and ignoring her struggles, "and wanted by many, but none of that counts when the one you want does not want you. I would be careful who you make your enemy Lyar." He shoved her away and proceeded to walk back to his dwelling. But he would leave her with something to think about.

"And just so you know," he said, his voice nothing but a whisper that only she heard, "if you had been paying attention, Arkean was going to choose Loa because he had no interest in any of them. Your anger is focused on the wrong female, Seer."

He made sure she could hear his haunting laugher as he melted into the darkness, wishing that her nights would ring with it.

●

There was a collective calm hovering over the virtually deserted village as Arkean walked around the great wall that kept their enemies at bay. It had been some time since the night meal meeting where he laid out his strategy for dealing with the Egyptians.

He should have been thinking over his plans or going over them with his brethren but instead, he was making sure there were no enemy forces close by. He was sure he would sense or hear them if he opened his senses. But just in case his newly acquired capabilities didn't work, there was a Guardian at every checkpoint in case of an attack to alert the village.

A strong alert Guardian positioned at the post ahead of him gave Arkean a nod. It was widespread knowledge throughout the village that the King gave him command of their forces during this conflict as a test.

Arkean nodded back.

He would not fail.

Arkean knew from entering the Egyptian advisor's mind that the attack would come tomorrow before light. They thought to ambush the village and take him, Bode, Gedgi, and Quende. The four were their main target. Eyet was an afterthought, to be taken if the opportunity presented itself.

The knowledge that the Pharaoh was a strategist who had a reason for everything he did, was apparent the day Arkean was told of his parent's murder and why. Arkean never once thought that the Pharaoh was completely heartless. Yes, he sent his daughter to a foreign place to mate a Warrior prince to keep the peace, but such arrangements were common.

Arkean would have his chance to work through his hate for the Pharaoh sooner than he thought. That the mere man included his friends in his bid for more power was a mistake. Now the Pharaoh not only had to face him but now his friends as well. He and his brethren were prepared; they would wait in the wide valley that the Egyptians had to pass to reach their village.

There were other things Arkean saw in the advisor's mind that was bothersome. The Pharaoh planned to make them bloodthirsty war dogs to conquer the world. The thought was unsettling.

Arkean pushed the negative thoughts away as he came to the entrance of the underground tunnel leading to the safe caverns that housed the villagers during hostile times. The need to check on the women in his life was overwhelming. So, he gave in, expecting to only make sure that Cire, Eyet, Mye, Ivi, and little Hetu were safely tucked away.

Only, when he heard the whispers in the air it was apparent that slipping in and out without disturbing anyone wasn't going to be an option. He heard the hushed discussion clearly with his newly acquired unnatural hearing, so he moved toward the entryway using speed he rarely called upon.

Arkean came on the scene quietly and unnoticed so as not to rattle anyone more than necessary. Aside from the two guards who were supposed to be hidden from view, there were four women outside the entrance. Three of the women and both Guardians were all focused on one riveting beauty.

"Tell her she must not leave," Cire said, giving Arkean a pleading look as he walked up to them.

●

Watching Arkean was always a treat for Lyar. Her eyes trailed over his masculine face. His dark eyes and dark long lashes were so stark against the tone of his skin. Her gaze fell to his jawline that she wanted to nibble. She relished the thought of stroking her hand along his well-defined chest, over his rippling stomach and down to the very core of him that she knew would stand up to greet her. What she wouldn't give to have his long muscular arms wrapped tightly around her as he…

Lyar shook the thought of him and her being intimate out of her head and focused on what was happening in front of her.

Apparently, Eyet decided to leave the safety of the caverns, but Cire, Ivi, and Mye had stopped her from going any further with help from Arkean. Now they all were surrounding the queen in waiting, demanding that she explain her reasons for trying to leave.

Lyar watched as Cire took Eyet's hands in hers and pleaded for an explanation. Mye, the poor wordless one, just stared with scared concern. Ivi, the one who loved to give her opinion even when it wasn't desired, was talking over Cire.

Arkean watched them quietly.

He watched them quietly but with interest. That was when Syn's words came back to Lyar. 'You have the wrong female,' he said to her.

Did I set my ire on the wrong female?

Lyar really looked at Arkean as he watched the women. As if he felt her studying him, he looked over to where she sat in the shadows as if he could see her. She looked into his eyes, held captive by his burning gaze. Then, all too soon, he turned away as if he didn't see her hidden and moved to leave the common area. Only, he didn't get far before he turned to look at Mye with questioning eyes.

Mye walked over to Arkean and placed a hand on his arm.

Lyar covered her mouth with her hand to muffle the gasp that escaped her lips when Arkean gently covered Mye's hand with his own.

Mye?

He cannot possibly want that defective female to bear his young.

But the quiet girl was as beautiful, arguably more so, than she.

Lyar watched as some silent communication went on between the two before Arkean nodded. He left Mye as he moved over to the three women whose voices brought some of the other occupants of the cavern to the common area. He tried to interrupt several times but none of the women acknowledged him.

Lyar watched as Arkean's frustrations grew, then finally, he waved his hand. The air around the women visibly rippled like waves in the river, then each of them went as still as the dead. Witnesses gasped and sucked in their breaths as they looked upon the three still figures.

Lyar watched their frozen stances with interest. Cire held one of Eyet's arms as Eyet was in the motion of turning away. Ivi held her hands in the air to stop Eyet from retreating. Even their clothing was halted in an unnatural stasis.

Lyar knew that Arkean was changed but he rarely exhibited his tricks like the others. This power in him was…it was glorious! She felt her body heat as she moved forward from the shadows to get closer to him.

Immense power radiated from him like an aphrodisiac, causing her lids to lower and her lips to pucker as she slowly moved toward him. A voice suddenly sounded in her head. It ordered her to stop, and just like that, she did without question. Her lids popped open to see she only moved a few steps.

What was she thinking? Was she going to declare her want, her need for Arkean in front of everyone here? And what was it that stopped her? She searched the room to see that all eyes were on Arkean or the stilled women who were watching each other. Only one set of eyes was on her, Arkean's, and his attention heated her like nothing she ever experienced.

In her mind, she heard the voice again.

"*I see the lust in your eyes. Will you claim me in front of them all, Oracle?*"

Lyar's body shook as his deep voice trickled over her insides. He was in her mind. The thought of it was both disturbing and thrilling, and though his question was an easy one, she again faltered in her response.

Her eyes fell away from his and she thought, "*No.*"

Arkean must have taken her hesitation for what it was— her denial of him—because she heard his voice in her head again.

"*I didn't think so,*" he said before looking back to the women he stilled.

Arkean touched Cire, releasing her from whatever hold he had on her. Lyar watched in stunned silence as Cire frowned, looking at Eyet and Ivi, then she gazed at Arkean.

"Release them, now," Cire ordered without flinching. The old woman obviously didn't harbor the fear most of the females, now including Lyar, carried for the four changed Guardians.

Arkean didn't hesitate to touch Ivi on the shoulder but it didn't escape Lyar's attention that to free Eyet, he just moved his hand in front of her.

Why doesn't he touch Eyet? Has he ever?

Lyar tried to think of an instance when the Guardian touched his kin's intended, and for the life of her, she couldn't recall one time. Was it Eyet who held his heart? It made sense—touching her would drive one who wanted her mad.

Like Arkean was driving her mad.

Lyar stood straighter, pushed her shoulders back and narrowed her eyes. A new sense of determination flowed red hot through her veins. She would have Arkean, and now that she knew his secret, it would be that much easier.

●

I need... I need...

Arkean closed his eyes as he bit the inside of his mouth, realizing he wasn't sure what he really needed. The thing was, he knew what he wanted. It was just that he couldn't have it and that was a fact he needed to accept. It was why he was willing to take the Seer as a mate. He was willing to take any woman as a mate. Yet, being near Eyet made him question his decision to accept their separate fates.

"Are you—,"

"I am fine," Arkean said before Bode could finish his inquiry.

It was rude but there was no point in the formalities of waiting to respond. His cousin's concern was coming off his body like little spikes, pricking at Arkean's skin.

Arkean opened his eyes and looked up from where he lounged, a small alcove in the women's common area meant for a Guardian to keep watch and defend if need be.

Bode looked a bit irritated but still concerned. "If you don't like me reading you, hide your thoughts and disguise your emotions."

"I thought I was," Arkean said as Bode sat down beside him. Arkean closed his eyes again and folded his arms over his chest.

"Try harder," Bode said. "Lette is inside the four of us, Arkean. That means we are all a part of each other. Have you considered that there is not much we will be able to hide from one another?"

That did occur to Arkean but he hoped that his secrets remained his and his alone. The fact that Bode might know how he felt about Eyet had his eyes popping open again, and him staring at his cousin.

Does he know?

"Before you curse the power Lette gifted us, I knew long before of your feelings for the princess." There must have been questions in Arkean's eyes because Bode continued, answering his unspoken, un-transferred question. "I love our great-mother as well but I do not spend every free moment in her dwelling, cousin. And, if you wanted to mate Ivi, Mye, or any of the others you would have told me."

Bode was right. Arkean would have told him which of the girls he wanted but didn't because the one he wanted belonged to Bode. But admitting the truth would be asking for death.

Arkean sat up. He looked down the tunnel then met his cousin's worried gaze. "You will have no problems from me. I swear it on the spirit of my parents. I intend to mate Loa."

Bode lifted his head from the rock wall as a low noise coming from the tunnels caught their attention. He gave Arkean a look that said, "We will talk later".

Arkean knew who was coming and apparently, he heard them coming before Bode. But not too long before. He could only hope that their conversation was unheard by their friends and even though he heard them coming he felt the need to give Bode his oath.

Soon Quende and Gedgi were joining them on the floor in the small space. Both looked as if they had physically aged some, resembling the young boys who left for the Maatii no more. In place of those boys were two males somewhat thicker in mass, and the boyish features the females loved so much had transformed into manly good looks.

Quende was now a roguishly attractive male who still loved to cause a little mischief here and there, while Gedgi's looks had taken on a more lethal appearance that dared, "Approach at your own risk."

When on a rest day, neither male could keep the few unmated women in the village away and it seemed that they enjoyed the attention.

"Rumors are floating in the air," Gedgi said. When neither Arkean nor Bode commented he went on. "Everyone's talking about what you did to Cire and the others."

Quende was hardly able to keep his question contained. "Did it hurt them?" he blurted out.

It didn't hurt but Arkean felt a small pull of resistance from them as they fought his hold. As for the women feeling any pain, he was certain from their bodies' responses that they felt none.

"No," Arkean told them. Arkean focused on Bode. Each of the women was precious to them both. "There was no pain for anyone."

Relief briefly crossed Bode's face then his features eased out.

A minute or so passed in silence, until Quende turned to Arkean, "Are you sure about the plan of attack?"

"We will face them as Bodai Guardians only. No using our gifts. If we could dull our strength…but we can't." Arkean said this as he looked to each of his friends. Quende and Gedgi nodded. He then looked to Bode who also nodded.

Each of them was aware of their enhanced strength and speed but they couldn't help that. They changed in so many ways but they were still Bodai. As Guardians they must fight with the skills they've learned, to prove themselves to their tribe and their King.

7

The sound of shouting woke Eyet from a deep sleep. She was exhausted and hadn't fully rested since her people began their attack on the Bodai three suns past. She rose from the bedding to a sitting position and rubbed her head. She was trying to make sense of what was happening when Bode burst into the room. He was fresh from battle and wild-eyed.

Cire rose from her bedding beside Eyet. "What has happened?"

"It's Arkean," Bode said, reaching for Eyet. "He is badly hurt and he will not allow anyone to help him."

Eyet had only enough time to cover her hair with a wrapping. She stumbled behind Bode as he dragged her toward the area where they set up wound care for the injured. Her mind was splintered with questions of how and what.

Arkean was hurt. *How?* The Four were so powerful.

Bode pulled her past several rooms where injured Guardians were being cared for. She was up most of the night caring for the wounded and now someone she cared for was hurt. The severity of that information made her get her feet under her and she was almost rushing past Bode only to be blocked at the entrance to the room Arkean was in.

Lyar stood in front of the room with her hands clutched in prayer and an angry grimace on her face. "You must allow us to help him," Lyar said to Bode.

With a wave of Bode's hand, Lyar was pushed aside by some unseen force. "It's him keeping you out, not me," Bode said as they stood at the entrance of the room.

Eyet's determination to help wavered slightly. He was able to keep people out of the room in his injured state? She stared at the doorway. The entrance to the room was visible but the room wasn't. She could see nothing beyond the entryway as if the room had…disappeared.

"My Gods," Cire said as she rushed up behind them.

Cire covered her mouth and said something Eyet couldn't make out. Eyet didn't know that Cire was even behind them.

"He…Arkean is doing this?" the great-mother asked.

"He is but I don't know how or even why only some can pass through his barrier." Bode tightened his grip on Eyet's hand and looked at her. "Will you help him?"

"I…what if he doesn't allow me inside?" Eyet asked, nervously.

"He will. I know he will if you are willing to help."

Lyar stepped back in the way, angrier as she cut her eyes at Eyet. "He needs his people to help him, not the very outsider whose sire gave orders to hurt him."

Bode gave Lyar a look so full of venom that she backed up a step.

"Please Bode," Eyet said, pulling his attention back to her. "Take me to him."

Bode's angry look softened when he looked to Eyet. He nodded then moved slowly forward a step, pulling Eyet along.

A wave of nausea overcame Eyet as they moved through a barrier of some sort that felt like thickened air. Once on the other side, it took Eyet a short time to get her bearings. When she could breathe without wanting to spill the contents of her stomach, she righted herself.

The room was quiet and cold. Torches on the wall lit the room but seemed to provide no heat. On the bedding, she saw Arkean lying face down.

Eyet rushed to his side. It was clear that he'd been cleaned of the battle and covered with fresh linen. Arkean's eyes were closed and his face clear of worry. He looked as if he was sleeping peacefully, and there was no indication that harm had come to him.

Eyet slowly pulled down the sheet, exposing a long thick bandage that began just under his shoulder bone and stopped just above his waist. Peeling back the blood-soaked bandage, she was faced with a red, angry deep wound.

"Who cleaned him?" she whispered. Someone had taken great care to clean him thoroughly.

"I did," Bode answered. His voice was low. "But I know nothing of caring for the wound. He prevents all but me, Quende and Gedgi from entering so no other care has been given." Bode stepped closer, touching Arkean's shoulder. "We have tried to heal him but it will not work."

For the first time since being awakened by her future mate, Eyet examined Bode. His hands and wrists were clean yet the rest of him was covered in dirt, wounds, and scars. Some were thick and bleeding while others looked months older; some even looked healed but none looked as seamless as the scars she saw The Four heal on some of the other Bodai Guardians.

Were they immune to each other's abilities?

Her attention once again was on Arkean. Why wasn't he allowing the other healers inside to help him? But it didn't matter now. Now, she needed to do what she could to do to help Arkean. She covered his wound back up then told Bode what she needed. Soon she was alone with her patient.

Eyet had never been alone with Arkean before. And if she was she would have never had the nerve to touch him. They only touched once. Not because she didn't have an urge to, but because she assumed he never wanted to touch her. During that one time, she initiated contact with the boy he once was. Then, she was a misplaced child in a foreign land with no one to relay her pain too.

Except there *had* been someone, a boy named Arkean. His family's tale was told to her by a nursemaid who revered a great warrior and who was still loyal to her uncle, the Pharaoh Eyet's father murdered and replaced. When she was a small child, Eyet thought the tale was a mere story her father wanted his children told, to garner their fear and allegiance. As she grew, Eyet realized his cruelty wasn't a farce and the stories her nursemaid told her were lessons as well as warnings.

So, when she arrived in the Bodai village full of strangers, Eyet felt alone. Even with the lovely Cire, who had once been of her people, caring for her the place seemed foreign and scary. It wasn't until she laid eyes on the handsome boy in Cire's common area who introduced himself as Arkean, that she felt a kindred spirit.

Over the years, she wondered what happened to the beautiful babe her nursemaid spoke of, the son of her Aunt and the Bodai warrior who was murdered. She once wondered if her father killed the babe or had he released the babe to his people like the story told?

Then she discovered the story was true and the boy, Arkean, was standing in front of her. And he was a young warrior and more beautiful than the image her mind conjured from her nurse maid's stories. He was tall, his skin smooth, and his lashes were long and dark. Instead of the shaven heads her people wore or the long hair his people preferred, his was cut close. His light brown eyes sparkled but not with the light of an innocent child but with the knowledge of someone far beyond in years.

After spending hours with her in silence that first day, as if he was accustomed to quiet or even enjoyed it, Arkean got up to leave. She could think of nothing to say to him for his kindness. There were no words she could use to apologize for the pain her father caused him. He was just as misplaced as she was—a child with no place to belong, and the thought that there was no place that would truly be home for either of them settled inside her just then. They were kindred spirits, affected by the same man's need for power.

There was no doubt in her mind that Arkean knew whose daughter she was, and still, he was nice to her. No one was ever nice to her without reason. The slaves were conditioned to work and serve without complaint. Her court feared her father. The Bodai needed her to breed more girl children and warriors for their tribe. But the boy who once stood before her and offered his friendship, wanted nothing in return. He should have hated her for the very blood that moved through her veins.

Now he lay wounded and possibly dying.

Eyet trailed a shaky finger over his brow and down the side of his face.

Arkean's eyes sprang open, and before she could move her fingers from his face he grabbed her wrist. He moved so fast she screamed before she could stop herself.

●

Lyar stood facing King Obade in his private chambers in the caverns. It was decorated somewhat like his throne room but on a smaller scale. Syn was beside her, speaking his concerns, though carefully. The Commander stood beside Syn in silence.

Lyar decided to listen as well, for now.

"They praise him well," King Obade said proudly.

Only, Lyar heard the underlying concern in his tone. She knew he wanted to go to Arkean, but their law forbade him to leave these chambers in a time of war. He had to rely on messengers, his advisors, and his kin for word of the happenings outside his rooms.

"The wound looks fatal my King," Syn simply stated.

King Obade looked to the Commander.

"Several attempts were made by the prince, Quende, and Gedgi to heal the wound but they were unsuccessful. None have survived with this type of damage."

The King lowered his head.

The Commander straightened and went on, "Arkean fought like no other I have seen in battle my King. I am proud to report that in the three days past we have battled, he alone took down more of the enemy than anyone else. He was protecting Bode from a barrage of arrows. He cut those arrows down as three of the enemy soldiers attacked him at the same time. He slew them all after being injured, only to fall to one knee when they lay at his feet."

"Who looks after him?" the King asked. He rubbed his hand over his staff.

"There is an unseen wall that restricts anyone from entering the room he was placed in. Only Bode and the other two of The Four seem to be able to enter without issue. I believe Bode restricts others," Syn offered.

Lyar said nothing to contradict the Ika's—medicine man's—assessment even though she knew he was wrong. It was Arkean who kept them at bay, and as for the Guardian succumbing to his wounds; she would bet her good name that was wrong as well.

Someone close to death could never gather that much strength to keep others away. She wanted to laugh at Syn and the Commander. They both wanted her Guardian dead. At least the fat bastard Syn didn't degrade himself by praising Arkean like the Commander. Syn wanted Arkean gone. It was the only way to assure he kept his position that the young Guardians were surely taking for their own, knowingly or not.

What the Commander spoke of Arkean's prowess in battle was the truth. Wounded Guardians and those who rotated out of the battle to rest, spoke of nothing but Arkean and his three companions. But Arkean was given most of the glory.

"They chant his name," Syn said.

Lyar knew she chose well and all she had to do to have him was to get rid of Eyet, permanently.

"They chant his name," the King said in a whisper to himself.

Lyar knew then that Syn found an opening to plant his poison seed.

"That is the only name they have been chanting for hours my King," Syn said with a partial grin.

The King looked to them, then frowned. Syn was smart and it seemed to Lyar that the King wasn't sure how he felt about Arkean surpassing his own son's glory, or his for that matter. Men were so foolish and easily swayed. She knew this from personal experience; to be turned against a loved one usually took torrid promises from one such as herself, but the seed of jealousy could also do that.

It would appear that Syn found his weapon against The Four.

"Inform Bode to allow their great-mother in the room to say her goodbyes to Arkean. He will have the sendoff of a great commander," the King said to her as he waved them away.

●

Eyet pulled hard, and though his grip on her wrist wasn't a painful hold, she was scared. Arkean's eyes were glowing. The air in the room seemed thicker, making it difficult to breathe. Her scream had already faded and the room was eerily silent with only the beating of her heart for security.

"Please Arkean, do not hurt me," Eyet begged when she found her voice.

"How could he ever hurt what he treasures most?" Bode asked as he stepped into the room, easily bypassing the barrier.

Relief and hope had Eyet looking over her shoulder to face Bode. He placed baskets of goods on the floor then made his way to them. Confused by his words and still scared, she continued to struggle in Arkean's grasp.

"Calm yourself Eyet. Arkean would die sooner than hurt you."

Bode lowered on his haunches so that he was face to face with Arkean, who had his head lifted and was blankly staring at Eyet with glowing eyes. Moments passed in silence, then Arkean turned his gleaming gaze on Bode, slowly let go of Eyet's wrist, then lay his head back down and closed his eyes.

"How…how did you get him to release me?"

Bode stood and went to the supplies. He lifted a basket, handing it to her. "I told him that someone he trusted was here to help him and that because you were able to cross his barrier it must mean that you mean him no harm."

She shook her head, "You said nothing. I heard nothing."

"*He heard me just as you do now.*" Bode transferred as he looked at her.

Eyet took several steps back, dropping the basket. His mouth didn't move, yet he spoke words to her. "But, your mouth..."

"Eyet, you need to work through your fears if you are to become a royal bride. I am changed and so is Arkean but we are still the same males and friends you have come to know. Will you help him or shall I convince him to let Lyar inside this room?" He turned toward the barrier then looked back at her. "Lyar is very eager to lay hands on him."

Why that tidbit of information made the fine hairs on her neck standing on end she didn't know but they were. Eyet noticed the interest in the Seer's eyes whenever she watched Arkean. Cire also noticed as well and made no secret of how she disapproved of the Seer's attention to her great son, speaking her disapproval to Ivi, Mye, and Eyet in the past.

Eyet bent down and picked up the supplies that fell from the basket when she dropped it. She stood, squared her shoulders, and went to where Arkean lay unmoving. Only for the friendship, she held dear, she would help Arkean. Her decision had nothing to do with the fact that the thought of the Seer touching him in any way made her want to grind her teeth to dust.

A sound of sloshing water caused Eyet to turn her attention to Bode. The big smile on his face made her want to scratch his eyes out. What was he smiling about anyway? Instead of turning to violence, she asked him to hand her the warm water he brought and she went to work.

"I must return to battle," Bode said, coming to his feet.

What, wait...

Eyet cleaned Arkean wound as best she could. The bleeding stopped and she placed a concoction of healing herbs on the raw skin and wrapped it tightly with Bode's help. It was a bad wound and it amazed her that Arkean survived this long with it. He was strong though, and as a testament to that, the wound looked as if it was healing itself by the time she got around to wrapping it.

Now she was done and Bode was leaving.

"Someone should stay and watch him," Eyet said as she gathered the supplies she used and placed them in the basket.

Bode lifted another basket and handed it to her. She had to drop some items in the other basket to take it.

"That is why I am leaving you here." He pointed to the basket she held. "There is food and drinking water in there. Enough for the both of you should he wake." He looked at the barrier then. "No one will be able to come inside and I advise you not to leave." He moved toward the barrier.

"You would leave me, your intended, here alone with another male?" she asked. Her questioning gaze turned into a scowl.

Bode turned to face her. "As I've said before Eyet, he will never hurt you. Will you stay and aid him?"

It wasn't a good idea but she nodded absently anyway. Bode trusted her to care for his kin and she would.

"No one will hear or see inside this room as long as he maintains the barrier, and he will. Please do whatever you need to make him comfortable. I've brought you enough to eat, and if you must leave, return as soon as you can. He will allow you back inside. When he wakes, tell him that I have returned to battle."

Did he know for certain that Arkean will recover? How did he know?

Eyet nodded again as Bode left.

Finding herself alone in the room with Arkean once again, Eyet could not ignore the pull he had on her. It was easy to give in and not fight her need to touch him now that there was no one around and he was…well, unconscious.

As she moved to where he lay she looked over her shoulder. Though she could not see the barrier, Eyet knew it was still there because she could not see past the entryway.

Arkean remained still and made no sound while she tended his wound. She was sure it was painful; she saw males with lesser wounds cry like babes, but he laid unmoving and soundless through it all. She was also sure that he felt everything she did because just like now, as she brushed her fingers lightly over his back near his shoulder, he shivered or sighed as if he enjoyed her touch.

Does he like my touch?

Eyet frowned. His skin was colder now. She quickly felt his cheek. Arkean shivered again. It too was colder. She turned to the entryway in desperation. She needed more covering. Only there was no way to get them until someone checked on them because she was certainly not going to cross through that barrier alone.

Sighing, Eyet took another deep breath and decided what she needed to do.

No one could see them and that was a good thing because otherwise, she would never even think of doing what she intended. Pushing her fears aside, she climbed up on the bedding beside him and snuggled into his body.

Eyet stared into his profile.

Arkean was absolutely…the most gorgeous, kindest male she ever met. She moved closer, allowing her leg to brush against his. He shivered again so she moved closer until her body was pressed against his with little to no space between them.

Her body was aware of his on all levels and she couldn't help but wonder how it would feel to belong to Arkean. It was foolish to think such things. Although Bode had not claimed her, she was his. Plus, Arkean all but treated her like a duty instead of a female. He rarely spoke to her but often came to visit Cire so she always got to see him. She was grateful he hadn't yet killed her, considering what her father did to him.

Though, the thought of killing me might have crossed his mind.

No, she could never be his, because every time he looked at her and their eyes met, his expression hardened and he looked away. He most likely hated her but he was cordial because he was a male of worth.

Eyet was surprised to admit to herself that she wished things were different. That she was his and he was hers. That her father hadn't murdered his family. She closed her eyes and wished that he felt the way she felt since he introduced himself that very first day.

A single tear rolled down her face but she quickly shed her sudden sadness and took pleasure in the fact that she was closer to Arkean than she ever was before. With a satisfied smile on her face, exhaustion took over and Eyet closed her eyes.

8

The delicate, delectable scent that was all Eyet and the comfort of her softness were wrapped around him like a warm covering on a chilly day. On some basic level, he sensed her when she first approached with Bode. He should not have let her inside the room but he was in so much pain that he wanted her near.

His guilt was ever present even in this altered state of consciousness.

Bode must have known that Eyet's presence would help him somehow.

That Bode did know and brought her anyway should bother Arkean, and it did, but he could not deny that Eyet being near had helped him mentally.

Arkean pulled himself out of the healing sleep the severe wound forced him into. The first thing he did was appreciate the reality that Eyet's soft delicious body was next to his. No, not next to his; Eyet was asleep in his arms.

They lay on their sides, facing each other. Her head was nestled on his upper arm and chest. Her long body pressed snug against his. Arkean's other arm rested around her waist. His face was inches from hers, so close that their lips were almost touching.

Without thinking, he secured his arm around her waist, preventing any sudden retreats on her part. She was where he always wanted her, in his arms, and he never wanted to let her go. She smelled like clouds and dreams and he wanted to melt into what made her…her. Those sweet parted lips of hers pulled him in and his pulse quickened. Dismissing the warning in the back of his mind, the one that screamed that Eyet belonged to Bode, he eased forward slowly until he felt the slight brush of her lips.

He pulled back some to reflect. The feather touch of their first kiss sent sparks through his entire body.

Eyet must have felt it too, or at least he hoped she did because her eyes opened and she sucked in a breath. She peered at him for several heartbeats but didn't move to get away. Not that she could. When her tongue swept over her lips Arkean's reins snapped. There was no stopping him now. His suppressed desire had come to a head.

Not even the Egyptian Gods could have stopped Arkean as he delved into another kiss with unbridled passion.

Eyet moaned in his mouth and Arkean savored the light vibration on his lips. He used his body to push her down onto the bedding so she was lying on her back. He moved his elbows to either side of her head, his body over hers.

Arkean felt her hair between his fingers and he couldn't resist the need to see it, touch it. He rose from her lips as he glanced at his fingers in her long dark hair. When she sucked in a breath he focused his attention on her face. She was panting, her lips swollen from his kiss, and her eyes were fixed on his.

●

He kissed me. *Why did he kiss me?*

Suddenly, without explanation, Arkean's strong hands pulled her up as he got to his feet. A wave of dizziness assaulted her as he effortlessly lifted her in a cradle-hold then placed her on her feet, making sure she was stable before lifting her head wrap off the floor and covering her head with it.

Is he angry with me?

"I just…" she explained, "I just wanted to keep you warm because you were shivering."

Arkean, who was looking at the entryway of the room, turned and regarded her. For a few breaths, he just looked at her. His expression seemed confused but he didn't respond.

Then he turned his gaze back to the entryway just as Bode came into the room.

Eyet instantly turned her attention to Bode who was staring at Arkean with a look of curiosity. Then Bode smiled, looking relieved.

"How are you feeling?" Bode moved toward Arkean, touching his shoulder and turning him so he could look at the wound.

"I am well," Arkean said in a whispered tone.

Eyet noticed that Arkean wouldn't or couldn't meet his kin's gaze.

"But we need to talk. I have wronged you and offended the honor of your mate," Arkean said as he turned and dropped to his knees.

Oh, gods, Eyet thought.

This was her fault. He only kissed her because she tempted him by lying beside him. Now, because of her, Arkean will face judgment and possible death.

Eyet was just about to tell Bode that Arkean did nothing wrong when a small smile, or what she thought was a smile, briefly crossed Bode's lips. Then it was gone.

Bode's brows rose as he looked down at Arkean then over at her. If he was angry by the confession, his handsome face didn't show it. But it was what he did next that surprised her most. Bode reached down and nudged Arkean to stand.

"Intended mate," Bode said. He then looked at her and asked, "Do you feel that Arkean offended your honor, Eyet?"

She shook her head. "I do not," she said meeting him eye to eye.

Bode smiled, but Arkean, who was now standing, looked at her with confusion pasted on his god-like face.

"Then, that's settled." Bode patted Arkean on the back and moved toward the barrier.

Arkean continued to look confused as he stared at her. She felt the weight of his unspoken questions all around her, making her look away.

"Come, Commander," Bode said, looking over his shoulder. "Your Guardians are restless and worry for you. We need you."

"But," Arkean began, "but this, I…"

Bode raised his hand to stop Arkean from searching for the right words. "We have many things to discuss cousin but first we have a battle to win. The enemy is weak. We need to finish this."

"I wish to speak to the Pharaoh," Eyet spoke up. Her voice was a little shaky but her words were clear.

"We cannot allow that," Arkean said without looking at her. Then he turned his back to her.

His tone was different now, harder. Where was the male who just tenderly kissed her?

Eyet touched her bottom lip as she stared at Arkean's bandaged back. She reached for his hand, brushing her finger over his to stop him as he moved to the entryway.

This war was also her fault and she wanted to put an end to it. She needed to speak to her father.

"Maybe I can talk to–"

Bode cut her off, "You must not leave the safety of the caverns, Eyet."

Arkean didn't turn to say anything to her as his barrier disappeared and he headed to the entryway without a backward glance.

Frowning and confused, Eyet felt an ache in her chest. One she knew well from maturing in the hateful atmosphere in Memphis.

It was hurt.

What did I expect? she asked herself. *Was he to say goodbye, to pull me close and kiss me again*?

When Arkean stopped and stiffened, she held her breath but then he proceeded forward and exited the room.

Gods, I have lost my good sense.

Eyet heard several gasps outside the room, then Cire's happy crying drowned everyone else out. She slowly made her way out of the room and looked at all the happy faces.

Oh, Gods, Eyet thought, *Cire was out here the entire time worried and I never even thought to tell her that Arkean was doing better.*

As if Bode sensed her guilt he touched her shoulder. "I told her that Arkean would survive. Our great-mother is just happy to see that I spoke the truth. Now get some rest, Eyet," Bode said. He smiled. "Thank you for helping, Arkean."

"I did nothing. He did it himself," she said, grimacing.

"You were with him. You did exactly what you were meant to do," Bode said.

●

Lyar led the way through a little-known narrow passage that connected to the underground caverns. She was a young girl when she first followed the pudgy medicine man through the tunnels one evening after dusk without him knowing. Her mother often told her to stay away from Syn, that he was a lecherous fiend who preyed on the weak-minded. But the man intrigued her then.

Then again, most things intrigued her then.

That evening, Lyar saw a man and woman couple for the first time. The act was rough and sort of animalistic on some levels, and that was not appealing to her. Lyar was astonished to see a mated female of a Guardian she knew with Syn. She learned a few things that night many dry seasons ago.

First, Syn gave the mated female a sack filled with fresh vegetables and meats; Syn promised the woman much more if she returned in a few nights to come. Lyar determined then that the act of mating was worth something to a male. Second, she learned that being mated wasn't as sacred as she was taught. And third, that it would be in her interest to pay attention to Syn's doings. He was indeed a shady individual but he knew how to get what he wanted and apparently his ways were successful.

"Are you sure that he wants me to go to…" Eyet asked, "to wherever it is you are taking me?"

The annoying female stopped, causing Lyar to stop and look over her shoulder to glare at her.

"Where are you taking me?" Eyet asked.

Lyar sighed. Her irritation level was spilling over. She needed Eyet alive, needed her departure to seem like it was her choice, and she needed Arkean to think that Eyet went to the Pharaoh on her own accord. That way, Eyet will be out of her hair and Arkean will see that Eyet didn't want him.

"As I told you, the Prince feels that you will be safer deeper in the caverns. The King and Queens have already been moved, so that leaves you."

Eyet nodded and they continued on.

If she strangled Eyet here and now like she so desperately wanted to, Arkean would always wonder where the fair-skinned temptress was, and would probably go off looking for her. Or he may sulk and never forget her, wondering if they could have had something more.

No, she could not allow Arkean to cling to the perfect image of Eyet that he created in his head. She would never be able to compete with a memory and such longing. He had to think there was no hope of him ever having the weak female. That she didn't want him.

Before yester-eve, Lyar would have wagered her life that Bode would mate the Egyptian. But the Guardian Prince had not only taken Eyet to Arkean, he even left the two alone. With Syn working on King Obade morn and dusk to encourage his mistrust of the four gifted Guardians, Lyar could not risk him learning that Eyet personally attended Arkean, with no one else present.

Arkean would surely be punished for coveting the intended of the Prince, regardless of the whys.

Lyar moved slower, seeing the small opening ahead. She positioned herself in a way so Eyet couldn't see around her to the males waiting for them.

●

The passageway began to shrink, making it hard for Eyet to see what was ahead, other than Lyar, who was leading her to a safer place. She let her fingers brush against the rough walls as they began to narrow in on her. Lyar was several steps ahead of her but Eyet had a clear view of the Seer's back until she stepped around a corner.

Darkness was all that lay before her now.

Sighing, but determined to do what Bode requested, Eyet moved forward. She noticed that the air seemed fresher and there was a slight breeze but she didn't think anything of it.

Why would she?

Eyet moved around the corner and took over a dozen steps then slowed when she saw that the tunnel opened into the night. Cautiously, she moved to the entryway, looking for her guide.

When Eyet came to the opening, she jumped back with a frightened gasp. Her quick movement was hindered by a hand that closed around her wrist and pulled her out, then pushed her into a pair of thickly muscled arms that belonged to a huge Egyptian soldier. The hand that grabbed her wrist was now over her mouth and a strong but thin body pressed against her side before she could take a breath in.

"Do not scream, Princess. If you do and someone comes to aid you we will not hesitate to kill them." The Egyptian soldier raised his brow, waiting for her response.

Eyet nodded.

"Good," he said. Then he looked at the soldier who held her tightly. The soldier lightened his hold on her.

Eyet's gaze searched the darkness frantically, trying to find something or someone to help them but no one was there other than her attackers and two horses. Her heart sank, thinking of what these men may have done to Lyar.

Eyet pictured Lyar's lifeless body lying on the ground behind her. That was until the soldier's hold loosened enough for her to turn her body a little more. That was when she saw the Seer watching her. On Lyar's face was a satisfied smile.

Puzzled, Eyet frowned. "You led me here for them," Eyet said. "Why?"

Lyar narrowed her eyes, "Because I will not allow you to get your hands on the male I want. I simply need you out of my way, Princess." Lyar turned her attention to the slender soldier. "My sum please."

"Tie her hands," the soldier ordered the one holding Eyet.

She was abruptly turned around. The muscled soldier began tying her hands but she looked over her shoulder to peer at Lyar.

Eyet shook her head in confusion. *What is she talking about*?

"A Seer cannot mate the King, Lyar. Ridding yourself of me will be fruitless."

Lyar laughed. It was a husky laugh that made Eyet uncomfortable. Then her laughter stopped and she just stared at Eyet for several heartbeats as if inspecting something.

Eyet stood up a little straighter, as much as one could while being plastered to a muscled guard and stared back.

"You do not know," Lyar said, then laughed again. When the soldier placed a small pouch in Lyar's hand she smiled then stepped forward as the soldier finished tying Eyet's hands.

Eyet spun around to face Lyar but the guard restrained her by grabbing her around the waist.

The slender guard held his sword up in warning to the Seer so she stopped and smiled. "You are so innocent it is almost sweet. Returning you to your father the Pharaoh has gained me an ally, but what I desire most is Arkean."

Eyet gasped.

"Getting you away from him, having him think that you returned to your people because you wanted nothing to do with him will crush the Guardian," Lyar said. She feigned a sad face and pouted. "And who will be here to pick up those pieces, huh? Me, dear Eyet."

The muscled soldier lifted Eyet with a grunt and placed her on the horse awkwardly.

Eyet scooted until she was straight. "Why would Arkean care what I think of him?" she asked as the muscled soldier mounted the horse behind her. The horse trotted in a circle, causing Eyet to whip her head back and forth to maintain eye contact with Lyar.

"Because," Lyar hissed, "he desires you above all others."

When the soldier tied a cloth over her mouth Eyet tried to move her head away but there was no use. When he was done, he nudged the horse and it began to trot forward, speeding up with every step.

Eyet didn't struggle even though she was being taken to a place where she no longer belonged. An advisor to the Bodai Royals betrayed them and her for reward. And Lyar's motivation was to rid herself of a rival for the heart of Arkean…who Lyar thought desired her.

With her moving further away from the Bodai village, Eyet's mind filled with many thoughts.

What if Lyar's right? What if Arkean does want me above all others? Dare I dream it so?

The soldier's arm protectively tightened around her waist as the horse slowed to move through the dense woods. Eyet tried to struggle then, hoping that because the horse slowed she could fall with little damage to herself and run, but the soldier was too strong.

9

A Lie Births Truth

Bode looked stricken as he stood in front of King Obade. He listened just like they all were as Lyar, who stood in front of them, addressed the King.

Arkean could read his cousin's and anyone else's thoughts if he wanted to but he would not trespass in such a way on his kin and tribe. There was no doubt in Arkean's mind that Bode was as shocked as he was.

"Did anyone see her leave?" King Obade asked.

Four evenings had passed since Eyet left, willingly or taken by force. The King was informed almost immediately but he didn't inform the rest of them until yester morn. It was soon after she disappeared that the remaining Egyptians pulled out.

Due to Bode's constant probing the King called the meeting so that Lyar could finally tell what she already knew. She was seen with Eyet last. Whenever someone asked her she would say that she didn't know much.

"It is possible but I am not certain," Lyar answered. "But I can say that she felt that she was responsible for the conflict and that if she left that things would be better."

Syn cleared his throat then spoke. "As it has, my King. Her departure has brought peace."

Bode stepped forward. His body was rigid; his hands balled into fist. "She would never leave here unless forced."

Arkean wanted to agree but his role in the meeting was more support than anything. He wanted to come and was grateful that Bode requested his presence. He knew that Eyet blamed herself for the conflict but was she so distraught that she felt no other recourse but to leave the Bodai.

Syn bent and whispered in the King's ear. Both Arkean and Bode heard what he said but neither of them let on. There were some abilities they decided to keep to themselves. Their sensitive hearing was one of those abilities.

"We're going after her," Bode said sternly to no one in particular.

"You would leave your people unprotected to go after a female you didn't care to mate?" Syn said flippantly. He straightened and cut his eyes at Bode. "Why?" he demanded.

Ignoring Syn as if he were not even there, Bode spoke to his father, "Arkean and I leave at dusk." Then Bode turned to Lyar.

Arkean felt the subtle energy that was swirling around Bode during the entire meeting flex in her direction.

He watched as something silently moved between the two. When Lyar gasped then looked to him, Arkean wondered what was said between them. Apparently, Bode didn't have the same reservations Arkean did about picking someone's mind.

His cousin turned to him and nodded. It was a signal that meant they were done here. Agreeing, Arkean turned toward the entryway to leave. Bode followed but stopped when Lyar started toward them.

Arkean felt a small spike of energy pulsed from Bode toward Lyar with enough force to push and hold her against the far wall.

There were some yelling and orders were shouted but Arkean tuned it all out. Stunned by Bode's actions concerning the female, Arkean took a step toward his cousin. Bode swung his angry gaze Arkean's way.

"Trust me, cousin, you don't want her hands on you. Say your goodbyes and let the others know where we're heading," Bode transferred.

Arkean was confused but he trusted his cousin more than anyone else in his life. That trust was what had Arkean turning away from an angry Bode, a terrified Lyar, and several shocked onlookers, including King Obade.

When Arkean returned to his dwelling, Quende and Gedgi were waiting outside. Arkean quickly explained what he and Bode were going to do. Neither male said anything when he was done which was unusual, but he had no time to study it. He had to address the other three heartbeats inside his dwelling. His heightened senses told him they belonged to Cire, Mye, and Ivi.

Concern was written all over their faces but it was Mye who approached him first; she was crying, they all were. Her hands moved fast in the signals they learned as kids to communicate with her. He usually had no problem following but she became frustrated and just began to cry. He got the gist of her concern though.

"No, we haven't gotten any clear answers. Lyar feels that Eyet left on her own to quell the conflict," he told the others while using hands signs for Mye.

Cire took his hand in hers. "Tell me you do not trust that. Eyet would sooner find our warring enemies east of us before returning to the Pharaoh's lands."

"You need to find her," Ivi said, taking his other hand.

"We leave at dusk," he told them.

Cire shoulders rose then fell as she exhaled a sigh. "Then we must prepare a meal for you both and prepare for your travels."

"For us all," Quende said from behind Arkean.

Gedgi patted him on the shoulder. "We, The Four, travel together friend."

By nightfall, The Four were fed and ready to set out. Many Guardians requested to go but Quende and Bode made it clear that they were to stay to protect and monitor the situation in the tribe.

They all knew of the unrest in the village. More than half of the Bodai supported the return of Eyet to the village. To them, Eyet was a Bodai. Others wanted to leave the Egyptians be, and then there was a small group who wanted nothing to do with The Four or anything that concerned them.

The King's refusal to see them off had the entire village in a buzz. Obade even forbade them to go after Eyet, according to Bode. After Arkean left the King's quarters, Bode and his father had words. Arkean saw Bode's anger reflected on his face when he came to Cire's dwelling for evening meal. Bode didn't say much about the conversation but he shared the basics.

It was clear that Syn had the King's ear and was filling his mind with envy and doubt, but there was nothing Arkean could do about that. He needed to back Bode however he could, no matter what. Retrieving Eyet wasn't about him or his revenge. It was about giving Eyet some sort of happiness; and from what he learned from talking to Cire this night, being with the Pharaoh and her kin wasn't what she wanted.

"We will bring her back," he promised his great-mother and all who saw them off.

●

Time and distance were irrelevant. How long it took them to get to Zau, he didn't know. It was Gedgi who suggested that they ditch most of their supplies so they could move faster. Gedgi and Quende had done more experimenting with their new abilities than he and Bode.

They figured out that their new bodies didn't need as much nutrients and water like their old bodies did. In fact, they discovered that they could go many days without food or drink. On the fifteenth day, they realized that their energy levels didn't suffer at all due to their fasting. Lack of sleep had little to no effect either. Neither of them slept and no one seemed slower for it. In fact, they ran almost the entire time, several times faster than any male or animal could.

For days, Bode ran at full speed, slowing to a slightly midlevel pace at times with them flanking him on all sides. Bode moved with a determination that Arkean had seen only a few times in his cousin. Arkean could only guess the Guardian was driven by his deep affection for the Princess.

Now they sat in a small cave a good distance from their destination city, going over how to handle retrieving Eyet. Bode sat against the wall in deep thought. He'd been visibly upset since finding out that she was gone. That his cousin was affected in such a way was even more reason for Arkean to make sure that Bode got her back.

Bode must deeply care for Eyet.

After Arkean saw them home safely he would leave the Bodai tribe.

As if Bode knew his thoughts, his cousin turned his gaze on him. "What's on your mind, Commander?" Bode asked. He chewed some salted meat they purchased from a vendor in the city during some scouting.

Quende and Gedgi looked at each other then looked at Arkean for his response. Arkean knew the two were communicating but he didn't know why they weren't speaking their mind out in the open. It was times like these that Arkean wished he wasn't so respectful of one's privacy. Curiosity was scratching at his mind. Were they discussing the plan, or him?

They all knew Arkean would never invade their minds and he chose to keep his private thoughts to himself as always. He was stronger mentally and most likely physically than the others, so he never worried about them brushing into his mind. He was sure that they would never try unless it was vital, plus he would feel the breach if they did.

There was no reason to put up a mental barrier to keep his departure from them. Besides, putting up a barrier now would only prompt questions because they would sense him doing it. So, Arkean turned his thoughts to battle mode and strategized how they were going to get Eyet back.

It occurred to Arkean then that he didn't want to hide or surprise the Pharaoh. He wanted the Egyptian to know that Arkean, son of Dwar, came to face him.

"We need no plan," Arkean simply said. "We have proven ourselves as Bodai Guardians. This day, we enter the capital city as we are, as Bodai Guardians with the essence of the Ilterians. The two joined as one. In Lette's language, you all know that the combination of what we are is called Coesen. The Pharaoh wanted us to come to him…we will, as Coesens."

●

As they arrived in the capital, the smells, sounds, and everyday life were just as foreign to Arkean as they were to the others. Nothing was familiar as he passed through the gigantic arch to enter the city of Zau.

Vendors and buyers did their business until they saw him and his companions proudly walking through the marketplace with over a dozen Egyptian soldiers as escorts. The people watched them with awe. Small children, some naked except for pieces of jewelry on their tiny necks and arms followed behind, laughing, smiling and playfully reaching for them. Older kids wearing the same coverings as the adults pretended to fight one another like the famed Bodai Guardians they heard tales of. They sang a song of battle they normally sang when a great Bodai Warrior won battles for their Pharaoh.

The Bodai was respected and feared, as evident by some of the looks The Four received and the way some of the soldiers walked with their hands on their swords.

This wasn't a social visit so Arkean had no reservations when it came to reading these people's minds. A quick invasion of several soldiers' thoughts told Arkean that the people did not know of the Pharaoh's assault on the Bodai, and there were no records of the encounter. Even if there were, the Pharaoh's propaganda and lies would make his side the victors even though Arkean and his brethren crushed their forces. In the end, the soldiers stole away with Eyet and their lives like thieves in the night.

The soldiers escorting them to the palace had no knowledge of the incident either. That made sense, because he and his brethren weren't in chains so there was no reason for anyone to expect that this was anything other than a friendly visit. Obviously, the Pharaoh wasn't expecting them, though he most likely knew now that the Bodai had arrived.

Both Arkean and Bode wore their royal collars and each of them was dressed in their battle gear and was fully armed. They were met by four soldiers as they climbed the palace steps. More soldiers joined them as they entered the palace. Arkean noticed that none of his brethren made mention or seemed impressed with the riches around them.

"Good, we should be feared," Quende transferred to them.

The Pharaoh and his mate sat upon gilded thrones looking every bit the role of royalty. They both wore fine white coverings. The Pharaoh's chest was bare other than a wide turquoise and gold neckpiece. His wrist, ankles, and waist were adorned with matching pieces as well. He watched them approach with smiling eyes but a blank expression. His younger Queen was lovely and dressed from head to toe with jewelry. Her face expressed more. She looked excited.

Soldiers stood beneath the throne platform, prepared to fight. Several males and a few females of the court stood huddled together with an assortment of emotions all evident. Fear, curiosity, and attraction were some of the emotions Arkean read from them.

Several feet in front of the throne two soldiers crossed spears for them to stop. Bode continued to move forward, causing one of the soldiers holding a spear to move back to allow him to proceed. Bode stopped right in front of the Pharaoh and his Queen, while Arkean, Quende, and Gedgi stopped right behind him.

The Pharaoh spoke to his court in his language. "I must admit," the Pharaoh said, smiling, "I had not expected them to surrender." He opened his hands wide, motioning to them. He addressed his court again. "Your Pharaoh's hand reaches far and wide my loyal subjects."

"Surrender is not our way," Bode said proudly in the Egyptian tongue.

The Pharaoh laughed heartily then leaned forward. "No, I suppose it is not. Then tell me, Bodai Warrior, why have you come to my great lands?"

"We've come to reclaim Eyet."

The Pharaoh laughed louder this time, looking from his queen to his court. "And why would I give my beloved, most treasured daughter, to you?"

Arkean balled his fists at his side and shifted from one foot to the other.

As parents go, the Pharaoh was the worst. When his son, who was just a boy, had shown too much interest in his throne, the Pharaoh had him whipped until the skin was stripped from the boy's bottom. Another of his sons he'd ordered beheaded for privately disagreeing with him. And the Pharaoh favored his sons above his daughters, so the females were treated even worse. They could not leave Eyet to her father's impulses.

His movement caught the Pharaoh's attention. They stared into each other's eyes, neither prepared to be the first to look away. And when the Pharaoh's lips turned into a slight smile, Arkean smiled himself. It was going to feel so good wrapping his hands around that bejeweled neck.

"I know you want to avenge your father and mother Arkean. I too feel that need, and if his death will ease the pain he has caused you, then we can lay waste to this place," Bode transferred as he looked over his shoulder at Arkean.

Arkean looked down at his arm that Bode now had a tight grip on. *Did I move?* Arkean asked himself.

"But think of how you feel about him, the man who has taken from you. Will Eyet be able to still call you a friend after you've had your revenge?" Bode lifted his head up at the Pharaoh who looked amused and was smiling even wider. "Once we have her we will leave you in peace."

"Bring me their hearts," the Pharaoh sang.

Bode released his hold. Arkean didn't allow the two soldiers who were dressed in foreign clothing, who stood in front of them to move two steps. He quickly brushed against their minds, searching for something redeeming. They were both unforgiving mercenaries from some other land. With a mere look from him, their bodies ignited in blue-green flames.

Every one of the other soldiers froze in place, not sure what to do. The Queen jumped to her feet, screaming as she moved behind her throne. The Pharaoh stared open-mouthed at the cindering ashes that lay at Arkean's and Bode's feet.

"Kill them, kill them now!" the Pharaoh yelled.

Bode's power filled the room. Not one of the men moved. Arkean knew that they couldn't because Bode took away their ability to move.

"Would you have all your men burn? There will be no bodies to welcome you into the afterlife. Think of your legacy, your reign, your lands. You know that we have changed. Arkean is not the same boy whose parents you murdered all those years ago. We are not fully of this world and we wield power you can only dream of. Look at your court. Look at your Queen," Bode told the Pharaoh.

The Pharaoh slowly turned his head to look at his soldiers, his advisors, then his Queen.

"They cannot hear or see us right now. And that's not all I can do." Bode sent the Pharaoh images of what would happen if he refused to give them Eyet. These images played out in Arkean's head as well. He could only assume that Quende and Gedgi saw them as well but they stood on alert as usual.

Bode continued, "What you see is a vision of what will happen, Pharaoh. I am not one of your Prophets or Seers. What I show you is a glimpse of your future should I let Arkean, unleash his wrath. See your pillars fall and all your history wiped away."

In the vision Arkean saw how he decimated everyone and everything the Pharaoh held dear. With his precious land crumbling in front of his eyes, the Pharaoh in the vision fell to his knees. Arkean, the one in the vision, stood over the trembling Pharaoh with a wicked smile. He pulled the Pharaoh to his feet and held him in the air. The Pharaoh's dangling body burned slow and hot. The pain he suffered was apparent through his blood-curdling shrieks and the uncontrollable jerking of his body.

Am I capable of this kind of anger, that kind of destruction? Why would I kill so many innocent people?

Arkean searched inside himself, trying to find the hate he felt in the vision but he knew what Bode saw was fact. He also knew that neither of them could see their own path. Their possible future was only visible if one of them showed it to the other.

Arkean looked at his cousin who was now looking at him with concern, so he hid his shame, swallowed the vomit that welled in his throat, and put on a blank face. One thing was apparent. He could never fully embrace his powers.

"What do you want?" the Pharaoh choked out.

Bode turned his attention back to the Pharaoh, who was staring at Arkean and looking a little paler on his throne. "I want what I already requested," Bode said.

"And any Guardian kin who still reside in your lands that wish to go with us," Arkean added.

"I…I can part with Eyet, but to find everyone with a Bodai blood will take time." The Pharaoh straightened in his chair that didn't look so regal now. "How do I know you will leave once you have what you want?"

"Our ties are broken after this day. We will never cross paths again," Bode said with conviction. "Now send for Eyet."

Everyone in the room began to move once more. They were a little confused, looking to the Pharaoh for answers. The Pharaoh's eyes were locked on Bode. Something silent passed between them that no one else was privy to.

Whatever it was, it was their private matter and Arkean wouldn't impose.

The wait for Eyet was almost painful for Arkean. A host of questions entered his mind over the past few days. Was she still alive? If so, did they hurt her? But all he could do right now was wait. He didn't know what to do with his hands so he clasped them to his side and tried not to look anxious. It took what felt like a lifetime for him to hear rushed footsteps. He saw the soldier first then his gaze fell to her.

Eyet's head was down, her eyes on her bare feet. She wore the customary wig and clothing that females in her station wore. When she lifted her head, for a moment their eyes met. Her beauty was still unmatched in his eyes.

Arkean could have sworn he saw a hint of a smile, but it quickly disappeared when she seemed to realize it was he who she was locking eyes with. He wanted to be the one to extend his hand for her to take but it was Bode who did.

Eyet looked at her father, whom she clearly feared. The Pharaoh said nothing so she quickly moved to take Bode's outstretched hand. Tears pricked at Eyet's eyes but she managed to hold them at bay.

"Are you well?" Bode asked as he looked her over.

Arkean's chest ached as she silently nodded. He didn't believe her and nor did Bode because Arkean was sure that his cousin and Eyet were speaking mentally. He watched as Bode's other arm slowly raised and gently touched Eyet's cheek. She glared back at Bode as the tears she'd been holding back began to fall down her beautiful face.

Arkean clenched his fists. He knew at that moment that yes, he was capable of every atrocity in Bode's vision. He wanted to lay waste to the place, and them for hurting her…for causing her pain. They all deserved to suffer.

"*Please cousin,*" Bode said but he didn't look at Arkean. "*Swallow your hate. Think of her…*"

When Eyet leaned into Bode's embrace, Arkean's insides sank but his temper did dim. Their being together was something he would need to get accustomed to seeing so he took in a deep breath and exhaled.

Everyone in the room silently watched Bode's and Eyet's silent exchange. Eyet nodded again and Bode's hand slowly moved up her face and to the wig she wore. Bode gently pulled the braided hair from Eyet's head to reveal a perfectly bald scalp.

Arkean now knew one of the reasons that had her so upset. Some of her people shaved their bodies, to keep cool and disease free. They believed that savages only wore hair.

For Eyet, whose future had been decided at a very young age, having her own hair was a part of her identity. She was one of the few here who was allowed to grow hair on her head. And they took it from her. He didn't need any more reasons to hate the Pharaoh, but it seemed the list just kept growing.

…and the pain in his chest was expanding with every tear and now sobs from the woman he loved.

"Don't cry," Bode said in their language to Eyet. "We can make you like you were." Bode looked at Arkean.

Does he want me to do it? To touch her?

Bode moved Eyet toward Arkean, silently urging him to take her hand.

Arkean couldn't touch her, not now, possibly not ever. He didn't think he was strong enough to let her go if he did. He stepped back. "Quende," Arkean whispered.

His actions were interpreted differently. Eyet wasn't even looking at him but her sobs became a little louder as she kept her head down.

Bode gave Arkean an understanding nod and led her to Quende who stepped forward.

Quende gave Eyet a reassuring look before placing his hand on her head. Within the space of a breath, her pale head began to darken with fine hairs. Her hair grew until it was as it was, a flowing mass of silken tresses that reached her hips.

Laughter coming from the Pharaoh drew their attention. "You back away from Eyet," the Pharaoh spoke to Arkean. "Your Prince clearly has affection for her; he is willing to go to war to regain her. But she repulses you, Arkean. This amuses me because it was you who she was first matched with."

Arkean frowned. *What is he talking about?*

"Ah," the Pharaoh sat back and smiled. "You wouldn't know that would you. My departed brother and once ruler of these lands had laid eyes on my comely daughter and decreed the day of her birth that she would be yours. You see, he loved your father like a son and you he treasured as his own. With his sons grown he focused on you, wanting you to have the best of everything; he wanted you to mate with my Eyet."

Arkean pushed into the Pharaoh's mind with no regard, looking for the truth in his words. The Pharaoh grabbed at his head as pain assaulted him. The soldiers tensed around their ruler, not knowing what to do.

"Help him!" the Queen screamed, dropping to the Pharaoh's feet.

No one came to his aid; their fear filled the room in waves.

Arkean's search was over in less than a minute's time. The Pharaoh slumped back on his throne as he panted, trying to catch his breath. The Queen's sobs overshadowed Eyet's now.

That pleased Arkean.

"Quende, you and Gedgi go with Eyet to her chambers to get whatever it is that she would like to take with her." Bode watched them leave with a soldier as an escort then he turned to Arkean.

What Arkean just did to the Pharaoh was only a morsel of what he wanted to do to the wicked man that sat on his high throne. Arkean would not ask forgiveness.

●

Arkean watched Bode glance over his shoulder at Eyet as Quende helped her onto the horse. She since stopped crying but her eyes were still puffy, red.

Arkean hated that some of those tears were because of him, but he couldn't change the way he felt. He could not touch her and that's why he was strongly opposed to what Bode asked of him.

"You cannot stay behind for obvious reasons, which means you have to escort Eyet home." Bode turned his attention to Arkean. "I and the others will stay behind and follow through with your wish for any Bodai kin to join us if that is their wish."

Arkean knew that Bode was right. It would not be good for the Pharaoh's health if he stayed behind, but he could not go ahead with Eyet. Nor did he want to leave his kin and friends here in this gilded civilized lie.

"You worry about everyone but yourself, cousin." Arkean touched Bode's shoulder. "How can I leave you behind?"

Bode touched Arkean's hand that was on his shoulder and squeezed. "Quende and Gedgi already called on the path of my staying behind. I checked theirs. We will only be a day's journey behind you. We will be fine. Check for yourself." Bode offered.

The vision was a flash of pictures in his mind but Arkean saw that no harm would come to his cousin or his friends.

"Being in this place upsets her. She's been through a lot," Bode added.

Arkean looked to Eyet who was looking down. *What has she been through?* It would be easy to find out but he would not break his self-imposed rule to allow his friends their privacy.

"Alright," Arkean said as he cupped the back of Bode's head, "I will keep her safe." He touched his forehead to Bode's.

10

The cave was dry but it was cold, and Eyet was freezing. For three suns set, they traveled together without saying more than seven words to each another. She thought they were friends but she was wrong.

When she thought about it, which she had during all the quiet time traveling with him, she realized Arkean never really said much to her in the time that they'd known each other. He was basically a silent presence rather than a friend.

I just thought…

It didn't matter what she thought. Arkean wasn't her friend. He probably kept near because she was going to someday be his queen. He was very loyal. She knew that for a fact. So, he fed her and kept her safe because he felt it was his duty.

A breeze blew into the cave and Eyet tried not to shiver but she did. The cold air stung her, causing her to gasp. Her teeth chattered but she quickly closed her mouth tight and hugged herself tighter underneath the covering she brought with her. She could pull the skins she was lying on over her but that meant she would have to lay on the hard, unforgiving ground. She could be cold or she could be comfortable, but not both.

While she worked out which was better, she realized that Arkean was no longer humming. She opened her eyes and whipped her head around to look for him at the entrance of the cave but he was standing above her.

Without saying a word, Arkean stripped off his weapons, placed them in a nook above her head, and stepped over her. He lifted the covering and slid down beside her and pulled her around and into his warm body.

"Better?" he asked.

Eyet didn't know what to say, and when she opened her mouth just to say "yes, it is better", her teeth chattered uncontrollably.

"Do not answer," he told her. He cupped her head and nestled it into his chest. "Just let me get you warmed."

He was so warm and he smelled so nice that Eyet might be able to forget how badly he hurt her by pulling away from her in her father's court. She accepted, even craved the warmth his body infused her with. She enjoyed the feel of his powerful arms around her, holding her against his chest; so much so that she closed her eyes and dozed off.

Eyet felt warm and safe, safer than she ever felt in her entire life. The low thumping in her head was so soothing. The gentle rise and fall of her head took her back to the days when she was a young girl, floating in the bathing pool with her sisters.

And that smell. Gods, that smell made her tingle inside and her heart race.

"Are you well, Eyet?"

That voice…I love his voice.

Eyet opened her eyes and peered up into a set of concerned ones. *Is he concerned about me?*

"I…"

Before she spoke the next word, he raised his finger and brushed a string of her hair out of her face. Eyet closed her eyes and sighed. When she opened them, Arkean's face was so close to her that she only had to move just a little to claim his lips...

Without warning and moving faster than she ever saw anyone move, Arkean was on his feet and several spaces away. He paced a few times then looked at her.

Eyet stared at him, confused.

"You can eat then we will get going."

She rose on her elbows and was staring at the cave's entrance. He was gone. Where, Eyet didn't know. Falling back on the bedding, she silently screamed. Why did she want him so badly when he had no desire to be near her?

She pushed herself up and stood. She ate quickly then packed her belongings and waited for him to return. With nothing to do, Eyet decided to see to her horse's needs but soon discovered that Arkean already tended to the animal.

She didn't know he knew how to care for horses.

The Bodai usually walked, realizing early on that the dense forest that bordered their village was no place for the gallant animals. But he cared for the animal as though it was something he'd done countless times before. How?

"There is a storm coming. I am afraid we will not get far before I have to look for shelter."

Caught off guard, Eyet jumped from fright as her head spun around and she looked up. Arkean was seated high above her, balancing on a high ledge of the cave.

"For your health, it is best we wait out the storm," Arkean said.

"If you think that is best."

She looked up in the darkening sky. There was a storm brewing but the rain wasn't what frightened her. It was the raging storm inside her that caused her to worry. The longer she was alone with Arkean, the more she had to hide how she felt, how she always felt. It was better that he never knew. She already felt the sting of his rejection once.

If he knew how much she yearned for his attention, his touch…

If he knew that he was her only tether to her sanity, that his presence melted her sadness when she was brought to the Bodai… That seeing his face with each sunrise was what lifted her spirits. That her dreams of him were what got her through the humiliating treatment her father meted out because the "savages" hadn't even wanted her.

If he knew how weak she was, that she questioned her role and duty every day because she wanted him instead of his kin, he would not only reject her for her betrayal, he might report her.

The Bodai were loyal. Their warriors were some of the most loyal, duty-bound males she ever encountered. That was why her father coveted their vow of service.

Sighing, Eyet looked up as the sky opened and a light drizzle began to fall. A few drops hit her upturned face. She blinked then lowered her head to see the droplets of rain hit the ground. When Eyet raised her head up, she gasped and stepped back. Arkean was standing beside her. She didn't even hear or see him move.

"Go inside. I will make sure the horse stays dry." With that, he left her.

●

Inside the cave, Eyet paced from one end to the next. It was midday and Arkean left out again, leaving her to her own thoughts. She felt sticky and unclean, and the rainwater looked so inviting.

It was mild out, not too hot, but the air was thick. Eyet reached out beyond the cave entrance. The water had a cooling effect on her palm as she extended it out of the cave.

No one will be out in this.

"I'll be quick," she whispered to herself.

Eyet headed for the pile of things Arkean brought inside and found her salts and oils. It took her some time to find a secluded area not far from the cave to unclothe. The rain cascaded over her head and down her body like an endless number of tiny fingers moving over her. She massaged her scalp and combed through her hair with her fingers, hair that was taken from her until Quende gave it back.

The memory of Arkean moving away from her in the palace flashed in her mind again. She didn't see his face because her eyes were focused on the floor at the time but in her mind, she was looking into his hard-brown eyes as he refused her.

Could she blame him? He saw her with her long hair. The sight of her in the Palace had to be, as her father stated, repulsive.

It didn't matter what Arkean thought of her. Bode was truly her friend. They talked often about almost everything, although lately most of their talks revolved around Arkean and Mye. He was kind, considerate, and caring. There were no sparks between them, no attraction on either side, but they cared for one another and would make beautiful daughters together.

The rain was slowing some so Eyet moved her hands over her body, mechanically cleaning herself. When she was satisfied with her efforts she bent to gather her things. A sound close by drew her attention and that's when she saw them.

Three males dressed like herders or farmers of the Pharaoh's vast lands were watching her. Two stood tall, dripping wet, while a third was sitting on his haunches, chewing on a long twine or stick.

Eyet gasped as she slowly rose with her belongings in her hand. She saw that hungry look in a man's eyes before, recently from the soldiers and men in her father's court. Food was not on their minds, and it was not on these males' minds either.

She turned and ran, slipping on the wet earth under her feet. She dropped her things to prevent herself from falling to her face. Her hands sunk into the wet earth but she gained her balance by pushing up with her arms and clumsily jerking forward into an awkward trot. She looked over her shoulder to see if they were in pursuit.

They were.

Eyet pushed herself as she made her way toward the cave. Her lungs burned and her breaths came out in gasps as she ran faster than she ever had to. She rounded a tall rock formation while managing to take in enough air to scream.

With her vision blurred by the rain, Eyet could hardly focus but her heart leaped with hope when she saw *him*. He seemed to appear out of thin air, a hundred or more paces in front of her. The look on Arkean's face was hard. His eyes were focused and frightening. So scary that Eyet felt the sudden urge to run away from him.

Eyet screamed again.

Skidding to a stop, Eyet fell to her knees. She whipped her head around to look behind her in time to see the man who was the closest to her, fly back. His body launched into the air with such force it folded inward, soaring high. She looked to one of the other men and saw him flying back the same way. The last man turned and ran in the opposite direction.

When Eyet looked back at Arkean, she saw the knife in his hand. His movements were so fast that she didn't even see him throw it. Or when he moved. The last thing she heard was the men screaming.

●

Eyet feared *him*. So, he kept his distance, allowing her a lot of space as she ate the rest of the salted meat. He was still on edge. Seeing her running toward him, unclothed, with those animals behind her…he saw death.

Theirs.

Even now, with them wiped from the world, he had questions. Had they touched her? Why did she leave the cave?

Gods, she was bare.

He closed his eyes and took several deep breaths that had no physical effect on him but were mentally therapeutic.

What really bothered him was that she suffered because he left her alone, all because he couldn't handle being close to her. Warming her up, lying next to Eyet threatened to break him. When she woke and her eyes were focused on him, with her body pressed against his…

She didn't pull away.

Arkean wanted to confess his desires when she was in his arms. He wanted to confess them to her the entire day, so he went on a hunt to clear his head. She should have been safe in the cave but she didn't stay inside like he assumed she would.

"You…"

Arkean looked up from the spot on the ground he was staring at and focused on her.

Eyet looked down at her feet. "You do not eat?" she asked. Her tone was little more than a whisper.

Of all the things she could ask him, she chose to ask about eating. "We need little nourishment since the change."

Eyet seemed to think that over for a moment then added, "Or sleep."

"Or sleep," Arkean repeated.

Eyet lowered her head and eventually took another bite of her food.

After he killed those unworthy males, Eyet allowed him to gather her in his arms and carry her inside the cave where he laid her on her bedding and covered her. He then went back to where he left the bodies. It took only a thought for the three bodies to burn to ashes. The rain now dissolved those ashes.

When he returned, Eyet was asleep. She slept for some time. Arkean knew there was a chance she would be afraid of him after what she witnessed but he hoped for the best. What he didn't expect was for her to question him about food. Though, he was grateful that she was speaking to him at all.

"Is what he said true? Do I repulse you?" she whispered, as she sheepishly looked at him.

Arkean was taken aback by the question.

Why would you… But he remembered the way she sobbed. The Pharaoh was still making his life difficult. "Of course not," he said. "Touching you…" Arkean sucked in a breath of air. "Touching you would not have been a good idea at that time."

She looked down then and said, "Why did you allow him to live? He has caused you so much pain."

They looked into each other's eyes for several heartbeats. He could not tell her why he spared her father. To do so would admit how much she meant to him. "You should sleep. We have a long day ahead."

●

Eyet watched Arkean stand, then walk out of the cave. She watched him until he moved out of sight.

She finished her food then wiped her hands. Slipping into the bedding, she shivered because the coverings were chilled from the dampness of the cave, but she settled in regardless. Her mind spun the events of the day repeatedly in her head and she found that with each playback she was handling things better.

She was so frightened when she saw Arkean standing in front of her with fire in his eyes, she collapsed with fear. To witness their deaths was terrifying. Arkean killed…every Guardian killed, but to see it was too much for her.

Clearly, Arkean was formidable. Knowing this made her feel a little better about him going into battle. But, Eyet couldn't help but wonder why Arkean allowed the Pharaoh to live. He and his brethren could have easily done away with her father and anyone else who opposed them.

Eyet was thinking of Arkean's reasoning for dismissing his chance for revenge when she heard him enter the cave. Her thoughts faded when she realized that he could have slipped in silently but he wanted her to know he was there. It was something so seemingly unimportant and most likely done unconsciously but it told her that Arkean must care how she felt.

She kept her eyes closed as he moved around the cave. It was hard for her to look at him without staring, so it was best she didn't look at all. Besides, the chill of the night was upon her again and she wanted to be asleep before it became too cold to fall asleep.

There was no way she could ask Arkean to lay beside her again.

Eyet shifted as quietly as she could to find comfort but stilled when she felt Arkean slide in beside her. Again, the covering separated them so she couldn't feel him like she wanted, but to have him touching her in any way was incredible.

"Thank you," Eyet said, sighing.

"I am here to protect and keep you safe," Arkean said. He was inches away from her back. His warm breath sent tingles over her neck to her spine.

"Keeping me warm is not your duty, so I thank you."

Eyet waited for a response but it seemed he wasn't going to give one. Then she was suddenly pulled back, closer to him. Arkean wrapped his arm around her midsection.

"No, it is not," he said quietly.

Arkean fell silent then, but he moved even closer. She felt his lips brush her neck. Eyet desperately wanted to snuggle back, to feel his lips on her skin. But she wasn't that bold and would have to settle for the warmth of his breath and his refreshing, intoxicating scent.

As if he read her mind, his soft lips brushed against her sensitive neck just behind her ear.

When he spoke, he sounded breathless and tense. "Tell me that you live for Bode's touch."

Her body didn't react the way she thought it would. Instead of stilling, Eyet found her hips pressing back into him. She shamelessly moaned when she felt his hardness when Arkean pressed forward. She heard him hiss, felt his hand as it slid up her arm, sending rivulets of pleasure to her core.

Arkean gently clutched her throat, raising her chin and forcing her head back so that the sides of their faces were touching. "Tell me to never touch you again," he whispered.

The way his touch seared her made her feel alive. There was no way she could tell him to never do it again.

"He desires you above all others".

That was what Lyar said to her. The Seer's reason to rid the Bodai of her was selfish; Eyet could now understand part of her motivation. Lyar was willing to do just about anything to have Arkean.

As he held her in such a dominant way with his manhood pressed and ready against her bottom, Eyet felt that she would do anything to have him in every way as well. Unlike Lyar, there was more than desire and want in her heart. Arkean had her love, but…they could never be.

"You risk your death touching me in this way," she said.

"I could face many deaths if you were mine, and mine alone, Eyet." Arkean traced down the back of her neck with his warm lips.

Her body shivered with need. Her breaths were short gasps of intake and release, her heart raced. But…she must end this now before she could not.

"I am promised to another, Arkean," Eyet said in her most authoritative tone.

Arkean sighed. Without warning, Eyet shifted as Arkean stood so suddenly that her breath seemed to be ripped from her lungs. He stood at the cave's entrance in a blink of an eye. He looked over his shoulder at her, his pain written all over his face as he raised his hand toward her. A crimson red swirl of air appeared and floated at Eyet, soon engulfing her.

Eyet watched as the tinted air spread over her body, cradling her in…warmth. Her body instantly relaxed as the cold from the loss of his body seeped away, but her mind was still reeling. When she looked up again Arkean was gone.

●

Arkean kept his distance for the rest of their journey, leading the horse as far as it could go into the dense woods that shielded his village. Once the horse could go no further, he untied Eyet's belongings from the animal and hid them for him or someone else to retrieve later, then patted the horse on the rear and told it to return to its home. The horse shook its head and trotted off in the direction they had come.

Arkean led Eyet through the woods toward the gates of his village.

Sensing his friends before he saw them, Arkean turned around. Out of the woods to his right Bode, his two friends, and over a dozen women, children, and men stepped into the clearing. Relieved, Arkean sighed. The two cousins were touching their foreheads together before anyone even realized they had moved.

"Timed it perfectly," Bode said as he stepped back. Patting Arkean on the shoulders he chuckled. "You look like you have the weight of many on your shoulders." He then turned to Eyet, reaching for her hand and bowing his head. "It's good to see that you are safe, Soahn."

Arkean watched the exchange with a heavy heart. Soahn meant Royal in Ilterian. Never had Bode referred to Eyet as royalty. Was his cousin finally ready to mate her?

He tried not to watch as Bode led her away from him but he couldn't help following them with his eyes. Eyet and Bode were face to face but their mouths weren't moving. It was obvious they were talking mentally. What they were talking about, Arkean didn't know.

"Arkean!" Gedgi called.

Arkean pulled his attention away from Eyet and Bode to regard his brethren.

"Some of our people would like to meet you. Some either knew or heard of your father." Gedgi stepped forward and did their customary embrace just as Bode had.

Behind Arkean, Eyet gasped then ran past him toward a girl in the front of the crowd. The two embraced then began to speak at the same time, smiling and crying. They went on for some time until they realized that they were being watched. Both girls' cheeks blushed red when they noticed eyes upon them.

Eyet looked at Arkean, her eyes glistening with fresh tears. The girl cried too. She lowered her head and said, "Thank you, Arkean."

Gedgi extended his hand out to a beautiful girl who looked very much like Eyet. "This is Anis. She is Soahn Eyet's blood sister."

Yes.

The resemblance was easy to see. Arkean greeted her with a bow. Anis smiled then looked to Gedgi who gave her a bigger smile in return.

Is there something more between them?

The fact that there were no obstacles in his friend's path to gain Anis' affection made Arkean genuinely happy.

Quende cleared his throat. "Are you going to introduce everyone else or just stare at Anis?"

Gedgi hurled a small ball of fire at Quende. Infusing a nearby tree with his power, Quende moved a leaf the size of a Guardian into the spiraling fire ball's path, shielding him and the people who were ducking and gasping behind him.

Bode shook his head. "It has been these nonstop playful acts between the two throughout our travels. Playing and laughing like babes. It seems that the idea of battle is the only thing that will get those two to focus."

Arkean laughed even though he thought that nothing in his life warranted laughter. His friends joined in and his problems faded. For a short while it felt like old times as the joyous sounds of their happiness rose into the clear sky.

11

The sun was setting and a great feast was being held in honor of their return. Torches were lit and food was being served. Looking over at Arkean, Bode took in the Guardian's rigid body language. Clearly, his plan backfired.

Instead of Arkean using the time he had with Eyet to admit to her how much he cared for her, his cousin pushed them further apart. Bode sighed. It was apparent that he was going to have to force Arkean to claim Eyet.

Movement beside Bode caught his attention. He didn't have to look up to know that Syn was leaning over and whispering into his father's ear. The Ika of their village had been feeding the King's insecurities ever since the Tandot and the reveal of the changes experienced by Bode and his brethren. Unbeknownst to his father or Syn, their whispering could be heard if one of them wanted to hear. And Bode wanted to hear. He also took the time to look into their minds.

"See the way the others flock to him my King," Syn sneered into King Obade's ear.

Arkean sat between Quende and Gedgi, while others had fought to sit around and behind him; hanging on the Guardians' every word.

The King lifted his head. "He is a Guardian Ika. His deeds are to be celebrated." The words his father spoke were true enough but Bode saw into his father's mind. The King was growing weary of Arkean.

"Some see him as an omen," Syn whispered, his tone was lower, more sinister this time.

For once Syn spoke the truth. A small group, mostly made up of elders, were uncomfortable with The Four and the power they held. Most gave them a wide berth, yet a quick peek inside their minds confirmed that they were meeting and discussing their options. A few even prayed that Bode and his friends would not return from their journey to retrieve Eyet. They saw it as a war decree and that eventually, the Egyptian Gods were going to retaliate.

Other, younger Bodai, viewed the return of Eyet and other Bodai kin from the Egyptians as a good sign. It confirmed that their people were major players now and not to be used for their strength.

Bode turned his head to look at his father, the King. Their eyes met.

"Your future and the future of your son's reign will be uncertain if Arkean remains here," Syn whispered, then looked at Bode. His chubby cheeks rose, displaying a wicked grin as the light of the fire hit his eyes in a way that made them twinkle.

A desire to rip the Ika's tongue out and smile down at him as he screamed and shook on the ground in pain had Bode smiling back. He would deal with Syn later. Now he had to do what he should have done many suns ago.

Standing, Bode moved to the group of women that were gathered together. He stopped a few feet away, dislodged his ceremonial dagger from his hip sheath then waited as his gaze found and focused on Eyet.

●

Eyet watched Bode stand and make his way over to where she and the other women sat. *It is time. I can do this.* All she had to do was move with confidence like Bode told her, and everything would be fine.

It was just that…her legs felt weak and her head was pounding.

Standing, Eyet watched as Bode took hold of his dagger. She took a deep breath, accepting that they were really going to do it.

Bode's eyes met hers, and she gave him a slight nod. Eyet looked around for her friends. When she didn't see them right away her hands began to tingle and she bit into her bottom lip, but then she sighed with relief. Cire and Ivi were late but they had Mye.

The claiming of one's mate was usually done after the Maatii when the boys return as men and Guardians but it was common for some of the men to wait to choose a mate. The males could claim a mate at any mass meal gathering following the Maatii by removing their ceremonial dagger and dropping to one knee in front of their chosen.

Eyet glanced over her shoulder to make sure Bode still meant to mate this night. He returned her curious gaze with one of certainty. She should have known he would follow through. Bode never spoke without action.

If he said something he never faltered.

It was no surprise when Eyet saw that Quende and Gedgi had risen and were standing in the middle of the circle on either side of Bode. She knew that they made a pact when they were boys; if one mated, they all did. So, it was also no surprise when Arkean got to his feet and joined his friends.

Bode told Eyet that Arkean would, and he did.

Eyet wanted to smile but her stomach felt too busy. She turned back to her three women friends. Mye looked like she didn't want to be there. She was conspicuously absent from their gatherings and avoided many functions of late. Eyet was sure she knew the reason why after questioning the others about Mye's health and no one had any answers for their silent friend's sudden solitude.

Cire and Ivi led Mye to the front of the onlookers' circle just as all the other women were lining up in front of each Warrior. Eyet half expected to see Lyar standing before Arkean. Cire informed her that the Seer hadn't been seen since The Four journeyed to her father's lands, but knowing the woman was still out there somewhere made Eyet's blood crawl.

Eyet looked over the women around her again and this time she noticed that for some reason the women were grouped together as if each hadn't decided what Guardian to offer her devotion. There were rumors circulating that the women may do something like this. By standing together, they were offering themselves to each of the well sought-after Guardians. Their odds were better this way, so they must have all decided to attempt this as a group. No one seemed to have any objections.

●

It was the first time since Bode kissed Mye that he was once again seeing her fully versus glimpses of her here and there. He had a mental image of her that he relied on, more times than he cared to admit, but it was nothing compared to her in the flesh.

And what a sight she was. Her hair was pulled back and knotted low so it hung over her neck. Her coverings left her arms bare but flowed to her feet hugging her comely curves. She wore only a leather tie around her wrist, something little Hetu, Quende's sister, made for all the women in the village.

Bode smiled inside when she stopped shifting and stood straight as a tree next to Eyet. The fact that his plan was in motion had him fighting a howl of joy. Mye wanted him just as much as he wanted her. He made certain of that fact before presenting Eyet with his plan.

Unlike the other minds he invaded, looking into Mye's mind made Bode feel like a thief. He planned to never take her thoughts again, but he already plucked out the information he needed. He smiled with that thought, not caring who saw. Soon he would have Mye, and by claiming the woman he loved, Arkean would have the one he loved.

A wave of Arkean's distress pressed in on Bode so he turned his attention on his cousin. The Guardian was stiff, his eyes unfocused and his dagger was still sheathed.

"Will you claim a willing mate this night cousin or will you back out of the pledge we made to one another?" Bode transferred.

Arkean turned his gaze to Bode. Those brown orbs were sorrowful yet lit with determination.

"*I have not forgotten our pledge though we were mere boys when it was spoken,*" Arkean said. He removed his prized dagger from its sheath. "*We will mate this night.*"

"A male's honor is the only thing he can truly own. It is a good male's weakness but it is also his strength. Always fight for your honor, live by your words, and you will die with your spirit whole." Those were the words of Kire, Cire's mate, and Bode and Arkean's great-father.

The words were what Kire lived by and what he taught his sons, Dwar and Obade. So naturally, it was passed to Bode from his father. Arkean was taught the family's mantra by his mother until she died, then Obade and Cire took over the task.

Arkean lived by his word, Bode knew this.

"Yes cousin," Bode said aloud, "we will all be mated this night."

●

He could hear all their heartbeats. He could feel their emotions running off them like water flowing over a ledge. It was like the wind's subtle push of anything light enough to be rustled.

For Arkean, it took very little for him to lessen or silence the sounds around him but right now, as he stood beside his friends, his mind was flooded with all the noises that surrounded him. He couldn't focus even though he was considered the rational one of their group.

All Arkean could do was blankly stare at the women, one of whom he would be mating very soon. He didn't focus on any of them. There was only one woman his eyes would seek out and he couldn't look at her. Looking at Eyet could be his undoing. Her mating Bode was going to kill him. Not physically–emotionally he will be lifeless and empty.

With a shaky breath, Arkean accepted his fate. There was no use in putting off what was expected any longer. He smoothed out the sounds around him to what would be normal, gripped his dagger, and rolled his shoulders back to stand erect.

There was no order in which they must choose. It was Arkean's assumption that Bode would go first. He was the only male who was officially promised, but to Arkean's surprise, Gedgi stepped forward with a smile. He kneeled in front of Anis, who stood with the waiting women.

Arkean wondered if she knew what it was she was doing when one of the women in the group told her to extend her cup. Anis was smiling as well; her crude cup design was that of a woman who worked in haste.

She knew.

Gedgi stood, lifted his wrist over the cup, and with a quick swipe of his dagger his wrist was opened and some of his blood drained into Anis' cup.

A second passed and the blood flow stopped and Gedgi's skin sealed.

Anis peered into the cup then at Gedgi. For a moment, Arkean didn't think she would, but the newcomer's smile widened as she lifted the cup to her lips and drank. It appeared as if she drank until the cup was empty.

Gedgi extended his dagger and Anis placed her hand over his fist. "Together we are one," Gedgi said.

Anis' eyes sparkled. "Together we are one," she repeated.

Quende moved forward. Kya, a beautiful young woman who acted more like one of the males than the women had Quende's heart from the moment she threw a rock at his head when he was just ten Sumas old. From that day on Quende said the female was his life. All he had to do was convince her father to keep her out of any other Tandot but his. Kya's father enjoyed an extra basket of fish each weekend as encouragement from Quende ever since.

The two performed the ritual and spoke their vows.

Arkean looked down. He couldn't watch, but he felt Bode move. It wasn't until he heard several gasps that he raised his head. He didn't find Bode in front of the group of women who had gathered for them. Bode had walked to the circle of onlookers and stood in front of Mye with his dagger in hand.

The quiet beauty's eyes were wide as she stared at Bode, then looked around at everyone who was focused on them. Ivi dashed away, to go find Mye's cup, Arkean surmised. Arkean was pretty sure that Mye destroyed it after never being chosen during several Tandots.

Shocked, Arkean could not believe what he was seeing. Bode intended to mate Mye.

Mye's worried gaze found Eyet as if worried about what her friend was thinking. So, Arkean chanced a glance at the woman he loved. Eyet was nodding as she openly laughed and cried.

Mye, who seemed reluctant at first, but was now armed with Eyet's tearful approval, turned her attention back to Bode.

Not being one to wait, Bode raised his dagger, stuck out his tongue and slashed across it, drawing his blood. He then pulled a shocked Mye to him and kissed her passionately.

Pulling back, Bode said to a dazed Mye, "Together we are one."

Crying now, Mye used her hand signals to say her vow.

Time slowed and Arkean's pulse sounded like a drum in his head.

"*Arkean?*"

"What is happening?" Arkean whispered to himself.

"*Arkean?*"

Arkean scrubbed his hand over his face. Was it possible? Did he have a chance at happiness? Arkean winced as a sharp pain shot through his head. Startled, he turned to the source. Bode was smiling at him.

"*She was yours long before she was sent here to me. Claim your mate cousin,*" Bode urged.

For the first time since returning home, Arkean openly turned to look at Eyet. She stood at the edge of the crowd with her watery eyes still focused on Bode and Mye. She was the only female not focused on him.

Then something occurred to him.

What if Eyet loves Bode and doesn't want me? Can she grow to love me?

As if Eyet heard Arkean's thoughts, Eyet turned to face him. Her face wet from crying, a shiver visibly passed through her, causing her to take a breath.

Arkean wanted to brush against her mind to know what she was thinking but he wouldn't. It didn't matter if she wanted him or not, he would claim her. There was no way he could trust her to another Guardian. He would do whatever it took to make her happy even if that meant never breeding her. Another Guardian may not be as honorable and might force her once they were mated.

Knowing what he must do, Arkean moved toward the women. Some of them sucked in an excited breath as he walked near them but let out a disappointed moan when he continued past them. When he stopped, he was standing in front of Eyet.

No one made a sound. Her eyes widened briefly before returning to their normal lovely size. Her breath hitched when he drew his dagger up and slit his wrist then held it over her jeweled chalice. His crimson blood poured into the chalice freely then slowed as he willed his skin to close.

All she needed to do was drink his offering to accept him.

Again, time slowed for Arkean. Forever seemed to pass as he waited for her to lift his blood to her perfect lips. His heartbeat slowed with anticipation and fear. Her eyes focused on her chalice at first then found his as she slowly lifted the offering to her lips and drained the cup completely, leaving a small drop of his blood on her bottom lip.

The urge to lick her lip clean pulled at him but he just wiped it away with his thumb.

Arkean's heart sped up as he raised his dagger in front of her. "Together, we are one."

Eyet blinked several times as she covered his hand and the dagger with her own delicate hand. "Together…we…are one," she said breathlessly.

Then she fainted.

12

Bode moved around the raised platform where Eyet lay. Her eyes were closed as if she was asleep or relaxed. She was covered in a thick, dark piece of linen that hid her form from her visitor's eyes. She'd been cleaned and her hair groomed.

The fever was still ablaze inside her, giving her cheeks a just-pinched look. Bode knew that Arkean wiped her body down several times a day and changed the bedding under her to keep her as dry and comfortable as possible.

He was thankful that her screaming had ended. It was difficult for Bode, for all of them to hear a female in such excruciating pain and not be able to ease the cause. It was driving them all mad, especially Arkean.

Bode turned his gaze on his kin who stood across from him; Arkean was looking at Eyet with his head down. There was no way to know how far inside himself the male was right now. Arkean might take any gesture toward his mate as an attack. Bode slowly moved his hand up and gently placed it on her forehead but kept his eyes on Arkean.

"I would never, *could* never harm you, cousin." Arkean raised his head and looked at Bode. His eyes were glossy and rimmed red but he seemed in control.

Theirs was a close bond. Bode knew of none closer. "I value you as well." Bode sighed as he moved his hand from Eyet's forehead.

There were so many wonders that were open to him now thanks to the gift Lette entrusted them with. So many things that he and his friends had been ignorant of were now open to them in so many ways, but some things were still hidden. All that knowledge wasn't known to them in an instant and understanding it all was difficult at times, but they somehow managed to make sense of things. Each of their abilities seemed to focus on what they found interesting. It was funny how Lette latched onto that interest, giving them the power to manipulate and use it. The mind was what interested Bode the most.

"How are the other mates?" Arkean asked.

Bode sighed as guilt infused him. He was relieved that Mye had not only come through what some were calling "The Four's mating illness" virtually unscathed but also that it lasted only three suns past.

He had a theory though. Both Mye and Kya woke three full days after the Tandot ceremony. Anis, Gedgi's mate, woke seven days later but was being kept away from her sister, Eyet, in case Arkean lost control and went on a destructive rampage.

"They are well," Bode answered. "The blood in our veins is not as powerful as the blood running through yours. Add that with the fact that both Kya and Mye are both Bodai and that we possibly share a close relation in our lineage; they adjusted to our blood quicker. Anis took longer. Eyet will take even longer to recover because you have more of Lette in you than we do…"

Arkean nodded. A hint of knowledge sparkled in his eyes.

Of course, Arkean worked the details out on his own. It stood to reason that Arkean, who was more powerful than Bode and their friends by leaps and bounds, possibly had a clearer, if not completely clear understanding of the way everything worked around them, in them, and beyond, due to their new abilities.

"I know a great deal but not everything, Bode. I keep most of this knowledge out of my head because no man should know too much," Arkean offered. His head was already lowered and his gaze was on Eyet again as his finger gently traced the still darkening mark that appeared on her neck just behind the lobe of her left ear.

Each of their mates now bore a mark in the same area behind their left ear. Kya and Anis had the same size mark that lay in the same general area but there's were turned differently. Mye's mark was slightly larger in width and in the same area but also angled differently than the others. Eyet's was the largest in width and angled differently as well. Seeing them in his head now, Bode realized that together the marks made…

"A perfect sphere," Arkean said softly.

Bode nodded.

A scan of Eyet's internal systems showed that she was in the final stages of the illness. That was good because she was thinner. Having to force feed Mye and praying she kept the stew and water down was not easy. But Eyet should be much smaller now than she was which meant that Arkean was aiding her in ways Bode couldn't for Mye.

The quiet was broken by Arkean clearing his throat. Bode watched as his kin nervously looked up at him again. "I should have been at your side to aid Mye. It pains me to know that my future queen suffered and I was unable to help her."

"You were where you were meant to be, Arkean," Bode said. He looked to the entryway as several voices gathering in front of Arkean's dwelling rose. "I am relieved to know that they have all survived this."

Whatever *this* was. Again, Bode had a theory.

Bode looked through the entryway, and though his view to the front of the dwelling was blocked by a wall and a corner, he knew who and what the crowd wanted. "It seems the females are out for our blood," he said, forcing a smile.

A slight smile lifted Arkean's face, causing Bode to smile even wider. "And our great-mother is the one who leads the charge." Arkean bent to kiss Eyet's forehead then straightened. "The barrier is lowered for them to enter if you will see them in while I prepare Eyet for their visit."

"I will see them in and calm them if I can." Bode left Arkean alone to tend to his mate.

When he came to the main entrance of the dwelling, Bode pulled the fabric aside and peered at the women in front of him. Cire, Ivi, Kya, and Anis, along with little Hetu, stood glaring at him with an array of expressions.

Mye stood in the rear with her head low.

Cire and Ivi had fire in their eyes, angered that Arkean kept himself and Eyet closed off from everyone for so long. Kya just looked confused. A brush of Hetu's mind told him she was just happy that she may get to see Arkean. Anis was a bundle of nerves and concerned for her sister.

And Mye...*his* Mye looked up with fear and guilt.

Bode shushed the women's questions with a low growl. Then said, "Arkean is getting Eyet ready to receive you but you must calm yourselves or he will refuse you entry." The women all agreed to his terms in different ways, Mye agreed with a nod.

He stepped to the side so they could enter.

Arkean walked up to greet his guests, giving Bode the moment he needed.

Bode grabbed Mye by the wrist as she tried to slink by him. Pulling her around and to him, he looked into her wide surprised eyes. Her body felt warm and soft against his, and the need to touch her all over pressed him.

"You are afraid." It was a question and a statement.

Mye cast her eyes down but Bode bent to capture her gaze and refused to allow her to look away.

"But who of?" he questioned. *"Arkean? Or is it of the illness that has your friend?"* He studied her for a moment longer then let her wrist go. *"Of me. ...you fear me."* Bode released her and backed away from his mate.

How could she fear him? Didn't he give her the space she required?

He slept on the same bedding but never touched her, never crowded her. Their union wasn't completed not just because of the illness that came upon her soon after Eyet fell ill during the Tandot but also because he knew the stories of her past.

Bode was there when her brother, Quende, came home to find their father trying to take her innocence. Bode was the one who covered her and held her while she cried when Quende challenged their father. Bode was the one who ordered young

Ivi to take Mye away to the safety of Cire's dwelling so she would not witness the death of either her father or her beloved brother. Even then, Bode was protective of Mye, and had in his head that if Quende died trying to kill his father, he would have killed the man himself.

"You do know that I would never hurt you?" he asked.

●

Unnerved by their proximity, Mye took a step back and looked over her shoulder. They were alone, she and…her mate. The others were with Eyet, she could vaguely hear them.

Since she woke from her illness her senses were sharper. She saw clearer, smelled the faintest scents, and felt everything more intensely. Also…she was hearing sounds.

Kya and Anis expressed that they were experiencing similar changes, but none of them wanted to share this with the men until they spoke with Eyet.

Bode took hold of her wrist, she guessed to gain her attention due to her getting lost in her thoughts. Mye flexed her fist and he quickly let her wrist go.

No, you would never hurt me, she said, using her hand signals. She believed that. He will never hurt her in the physical sense anyway. Bode and Quende were very close and that was probably why some of the elders were saying what they were saying.

Having a lot to say, Mye decided to mentally transfer the rest rather than using hand signals. Looking down at her hands she transferred. *"But I question the reason you mated me. We…you do not…"* She paused to think of the right words. *"You never touch me, the way a male touches his mate."*

Bode frowned. *"You have been ill Mye,"* he transferred as well.

Him speaking in her head made her happy. She didn't want everyone knowing their problems.

A subtle tingle at the base of her neck brought her head up. Mye frowned as she stared at him. *"Keep out of my thoughts, Bode,*" she warned softly. "*We are one and I would be your equal in all things concerning our mating. So, don't pick. Ask.*"

Bode smiled and Mye's heart leaped.

With a slight bow, he transferred, "*I would have you as my equal in all things, Mye, including our mating and my tribal affairs. Though, I have to admit that you are far above my station.*"

Embarrassed, Mye looked back to her hands. Never had she let someone get under her defenses the way Bode had. It was all so strange; the way they were a short time ago and how they were now. Bode was just another guy then.

Well, maybe not a regular guy. Though he's a Prince of their people, he and Arkean never rose above all of them as if they were of a better breed. Instead, they acted like everyone else, playing, fishing, and hunting with the others as if they were regular males.

It is often forgotten at times that they are who they are, that they are Royals.

If the long-ago illness that affected the females of the Bodai had not made their numbers so low, Mye would not have been permitted to stand in the Tandot. As it were, the female to male numbers called for some adjustments of that tradition and a few others, making it possible for a commoner to mate a Royal.

Even so, Mye looked upon the young royal as a friend and never as a male like the other females did. Her brother often followed Bode and Arkean around until he was accepted as one of them. Because of their closeness, she was graced with his presence often. But in all that time, never did she want him as she wanted him now. She never looked upon him and saw the spark of life in his brown eyes, the smooth power of his brown muscled skin, or the silky look of his dark hair.

Shifting her balance from one foot to the other, Mye looked down and focused on her hands for fear that she would give her desire away. For the first time in her life, she was relieved that she was unable to speak. The boy she once knew was all man now and it made her uncomfortable that she wanted him to want her…because she wanted him so much.

When she felt his finger on her chin she silently gasped. Mye forced herself to stay still as he slowly lifted her gaze to his.

"My concern for your wellbeing is the only reason I have held myself from you, Mye. Your experience with male attention and your illness has given me pause." They were eye to eye now. "But I should have realized how strong you are. Now that I do…"

He touched his lips to hers. The kiss was gentle at first then he eased his arms around her waist and pulled her close to him as he deepened it.

When he released her lips, she didn't have any idea how much time had passed. All she knew was that her thoughts were jumbled and her legs were unsteady. It was a good thing he had hold of her.

As Bode stared down at her, Mye could see by his strained features that he was affected by their contact just as much as she was.

"You should never listen to the words of lonely souls. They seldom know the hearts of the subjects of their conversation. Do not listen to all the talk. I wanted you because no other female does to me what only a look from you does." With beseeching eyes, Bode said, "And I hope that you accepted me because there is a part of you that wants me too."

There was no reason to lie to him. Even if there was a reason, Mye was sure she couldn't lie to him. Mye responded by using a series of hand signals.

His relief and smile lit his already bright brown eyes causing Mye to smile as well.

"And I only want you too, Mye."

●

The mental voices of his family and friends blanketed Arkean. Not with fear, anxiety, or hate like some of the minds he touched since Eyet's illness. No, the people in his dwelling had thoughts that were comforting, soothing, and encouraging. He felt a small pinch of guilt for invading their personal thoughts but he trusted no one when it came to his mate's safety.

No one.

He was grateful his three closest friends opened their minds to him freely, accepting his need to protect Eyet. Even the women agreed to his immoral invasion as a condition to enter his place of rest to see his mate, without hesitation. They all trusted him completely and it shamed him that he couldn't offer the same, at least not now.

"You forget that I was hesitant to let in well-wishers when Mye fell ill."

Arkean looked over his shoulder to see Bode lazily leaning on the entrance frame that led to the garden. His dwelling was a single round structure with only three rooms. The main room had two entrances. One led to the village and the other led to an open area that he used for cooking and gardening.

"Yes, but you did and you did not peek into their minds, Bode," Arkean said, then winced with guilt. He turned his head back around and focused on the boiling stew and vegetables he was preparing for his guests.

Bode pushed off the wall and walked over to him. "I would tell you that you were right but that would be a lie. Besides, I have no aversions to *peeking* like you do, cousin."

Arkean let out a chuckle as Bode took a seat on the bench next to him. It was nice to feel lighter, enough to laugh after so many days of worrying. He let his chuckle fade into a smile. "You didn't peek inside my head."

"I did not find it necessary," Bode said. He sighed as he looked up at the mid-day sun. "You've been protecting me since I can remember. There is no reason for you to harm me by hurting someone I care deeply for." He touched Arkean's shoulder. "You were not as fortunate as I. There was no one to be what you are to me so you had to protect yourself. It is why you are so careful with your mate. No one would fault you for that."

Placing his hand on the back of Bode's neck and touching his forehead to his cousin's, Arkean said with love for his kin. "You will make a great King."

The smile that Bode gave him was one of acceptance, but Arkean saw something else in his kin's eyes. Arkean would not peruse what it was though, being as he already questioned his friends' loyalty by invading their minds concerning Eyet today. Whatever Bode was up to, Arkean would trust him as King, the same as he trusted him as a Bodai Guardian.

Bode sighed again.

Though, there seemed to be something on his cousin's mind. "What is it?"

"I would normally not ask that you leave your mate's side but there is a meeting that we must attend," Bode said, then paused before adding, "though our attendance will not be welcome."

●

Bode tried to stay as calm as possible but it was hard to do under the circumstances. The meeting with the King was called by Syn and the Commander of the Guardians. In attendance with those two were four Guardians of high rank and three elders. Each had their reasons for requesting the King's ear but their goals were the same—to rid the Bodai of Bode, Arkean, and their two friends who returned to the village changed.

As he and Arkean came to the entrance to the King's throne room two guards stopped them. Never had Bode been denied entry into his father's throne room and he wasn't going to allow anyone to keep him out now. With a slight wave of his hand and a softly spoken word both men fell back against the wall and slid into a slump.

Arkean glanced at him with a raised brow but didn't say a word.

To deny the Prince was risking his wrath. Bode's wrath was legendary when it came to rules and principle. Though Bode regarded his cousin as fair he knew that Arkean felt that some penalties bordered on severe. For the most part, Bode felt this held true. Though he and Arkean were taught at an early age that if the punishment was harsh enough the offender would think twice before offending again, Arkean seemed to repel the idea that beating a man down would change him.

But...

"I suppose you have rubbed off on me," Bode frowned. "They were only following orders."

Arkean tried to hide his smile of approval but failed.

Bode felt a sense of worth because of his cousin's simple approving gesture and it made him smile as well. But the voices coming from inside took his joy.

"The women have been infected with their poison," Syn was saying. "We should have banished them when they first returned. We—"

"They are too powerful," the Commander interrupted. "I remember your brother's skill on the battlefield, and Arkean exceeds his father in every way. And Bode and the two others are just as fierce."

"But Arkean was injured," Syn offered.

Bode knew that Arkean heard it all, just as he did but his cousin didn't seem the least bit upset over the conspiracy. Yet, Bode was vibrating with anger. He told himself that he needed to stay calm if he was going to convince his father that this meeting was unnecessary. The four of them were not a threat to the village.

"Should we not be allowed to speak on our own behalf?" Bode asked as he and Arkean stepped into the room. He knew just who was in the room but Bode made it a point to look at each of them in the eyes.

Syn didn't even flinch. He just returned the stare with a smugness of which only the Ika was capable. Bode regarded the other two Guardians and then the Elders, who were made up of two men and one woman. Bode knew that the Elders' roles were that of witness but on occasion they were mediators.

After a quick brush of their thoughts, Bode knew the direction of their thoughts save one. She seemed indifferent.

Bode turned his gaze on the only person he hadn't yet, his father, the King. "When accused of an offense, the accused has a right to speak on their behalf," Bode spoke to his father then turned his gaze on the Commander and Syn. "But I am kept out."

"No one is keeping you out, Bode," said King Obade. "This is nothing formal. Some of my people have expressed their concerns and Syn and the Commander have been chosen to voice them." The King moved his gaze to Arkean. "And I will admit that I share in some of those concerns."

Bode listened to Syn's thoughts

The girl will not survive. What is she holding onto in this world? Once she dies no one will contest my words and things will be back to the way they were, Syn thought.

The Commander stared at them so Bode tuned into his thoughts as well.

He thinks he can show me up. I am a Guardian, a Commander. No trickster will take the role I have worked hard for, the Commander thought.

Bode picked the thoughts from his father's head next.

My legacy is on the line, the King thought. *What happened to them? How has it affected Bode?*

"But since you are both here, we may as well make this formal," King Obade said. He looked to the elders. "As of now, you will witness this meeting as impartial."

One of the male elders stepped forward. "I regret that I cannot be impartial," the man said. "I will speak against The Four."

The Four.

That was what some of the Bodai were calling him and his friends now. At first, it annoyed him but now he felt it made things easier for some to address them. He kind of liked being a part of their special club.

The other man stepped forward as well. "I will not be able to be impartial either." That didn't surprise Bode because the man was Quende's mate's kin. "Kya has suffered through the illness but is still herself, other than the mark she now bears. I would hear any charge against the Four beside them, as an ally."

Arkean stepped forward and raised his hand. His movements made everyone flinch, other than Bode, the elder Fin who stood with them, and the elder Yona who hadn't voiced whether to stand witness or to choose a side.

Yona's lack of reaction could mean one of two things. Either she just didn't fear them and knew they would not hurt her or she was resolved in her age and was too tired to care. Whichever the reason, Yona had Bode's respect.

"There is no need for allies," Arkean said as he looked at the King. "Uncle, I wish no harm to anyone, least of all you. We are connected by blood and that holds a deep bond in my heart," Arkean said, then waited for his uncle's response. When none came or even a slight change in the King's demeanor, Arkean continued. "But you have made up your mind I see…so I will spare you the guilt of killing a kinsman and take my leave."

"No!" Bode shouted. His voice boomed throughout the room like thunder, forcing everyone's attention on him, but he could not find a need to care about the fear he caused. He moved in front of Arkean so that they were face to face, blocking his father's and most of Syn's view. "We are of one," Bode told Arkean. "One nation, one people and you know this to be true. You also know that it is *you*, who is the rightful King."

King Obade jumped to his feet and started pulling at Bode's arm. But Bode was unmoving as his eyes bore into Arkean's.

The King spoke out. "What madness do you speak, Bode? You will be King. You are my heir."

"It is just as I said my King," Syn sneered. "He rules their minds. Arkean must be struck down or your legacy will dissolve, slowly by his tutelage or snuffed out by a quick assault by his orders. You and yours would be lucky to—"

The Ika's words were silenced as Bode swung out his arm and closed his tensed hand into a tight fist. Then he punched out with that fist causing Syn's body to lift from the floor, soar into the air, then slam to the ground.

Bode heard his father gasp and he also heard movement from the men in the room. No doubt they were trying to distance themselves from his wrath. He understood completely because, with the way he was feeling now, he wouldn't want to be anywhere near him either.

The sound of stifled feminine laughter filled the room.

Bode took a deep breath and let it out. "I have ignored you until now but if you continue your hateful campaign, Ika," Bode sneered, "I will rip out your tongue."

"He threatens the Ika." The Commander said.

Bode glared at the Commander. The look seemed to be enough to silence him.

"Stop this Bode," the King demanded.

Bode turned his angry gaze on his father.

King Obade recoiled. "You forget your place," he said softly.

"You forget your place sire, your role. You forget what is important!" Bode yelled.

Bode felt and heard when Arkean shifted. He whipped his head around, noting that his cousin was leaving. It took just two steps for Bode to close the space Arkean created. Bode grabbed Arkean's shoulder and spun him around. "Do not do this. Do not leave like this."

"Please Bode," Arkean placed his hand over Bode's. He gave Bode's hand a gentle squeeze before removing it from his shoulder. Looking past Bode, Arkean looked at each person in the room. "Eyet is waking. Once she is fit for travel we will go."

Arkean then looked at Bode and offered him a slight smile. *"Do not be angry. This is how it should be."*

Bode felt… He felt lost, angry, and sorrowful that he couldn't make them all see. Consumed with emotion, he dropped to his knees at Arkean's feet and lowered his head. "Not like this."

"You kneel before him like he is your King!" King Obade accused vehemently. The King grabbed Bode's arm and tried unsuccessfully to pull him to his feet.

With a flick of Bode's hand, King Obade slid across the floor. "Leave. Me. Be. Father," Bode said, through clenched teeth and narrowed eyes. "Will Quende and Gedgi be next? Then me…will I be banished as well?" His words were directed to no one but meant for all. "Yes, we are changed but we remain the boys you knew. Arkean remains good and he will still die protecting all of you," he spat. "All Of You. But you would reject him, us, because you envy his power and strength. Arkean is a—"

"Do not say it," Arkean warned.

Bode snapped his head up and peered at his kin. Nothing mattered but this moment. No one in the room mattered. "Why not? Why do you try to hide what you have become? What you have always been even before Lette's gift to us? You are the *just* one. You are a natural leader just as I am. Your skill with a blade surpasses all and I dare say even the great, Dwar. You are a born—"

"Do not say it," Arkean begged. "Get to your feet, Bode."

"King," Bode finished. "You are a born King, Arkean, son of Dwar. It is in your blood right as it is in mine."

Bode heard his father yell.

He heard when the Ika, Syn, chanted "Kill him. Kill Arkean and the witchery he has over the other two or your son will forever be under his hold."

Bode heard Yona scream and one of the elder men call out 'No!'.

The air around Bode stirred.

With his dagger in hand, his father lunged toward Arkean, who made no attempt to defend himself.

Bode had been distracted by his own thoughts. That was why he didn't sense or know what was happening to prevent it until it was too late. By the time he did realize what was happening he could only react. Bode knew that his cousin would die before he lifted a hand to his Uncle, the King, who was a skilled Guardian himself and trained alongside Dwar. Bode also knew that his father would strike true.

Seeing no other choice, Bode stepped in front of Arkean just as his father struck.

●

"No!" Arkean cried out. No one moved. No one breathed.

Arkean knew this day was coming. He knew that some would see him as wicked and tainted but this…

Bode shielded him from *the King*.

Arkean held Bode up as he looked at his kin's profile that was set in a pained grimace. Arkean could not tell it was from the injury or his emotions. Bode's hand was wrapped around the blade held by their King, their kin. Blood dripped down Bode's torso into his linen kilt, turning it red as the fibers soaked in the moisture.

In the deafening silence, King Obade's shocked face twisted into something evil. Then he stood up a little straighter and used his weight to push the blade that was embedded in the center of Bode's heart deeper.

Arkean was too shocked to respond but…

Bode's pained expression transformed into anger as he straightened and stood on his own. His emotions were so raw that they were projecting outward. Arkean felt the wave of heat pulse in the air and it was coming from Bode.

Arkean did the only thing his instincts told him. He threw his hand up in the direction of the two Guardians and hurled them to where the elders huddled together. Then he flashed in front of the Elders and the two dazed Warriors so quickly that one of them screamed. He turned his back to them and raised both his hands in front of his chest and braced himself against what was coming.

When the pulse of anger-filled energy released from Bode mere seconds later, Arkean closed his eyes and called on the alien power that the Bodai in attendance feared, to protect them.

In self-preservation mode, Arkean shut out everything to keep him and the people he protected safe. Then, with nothing pushing against his barrier, he allowed the sounds around him to return and opened his eyes. Beside the throne, Syn lay on the floor, his body charred, his life gone from him. Several feet away, the scorched remnants of King Obade stood like a statue with his hand still gripping the dagger's handle embedded in Bode's heart.

Bode was still, his eyes focused on his father's empty soulless gaze. His chest rose and fell with every hiss of breath he sucked through his pursed lips. His bloody fingers that were still wrapped around the blade were no doubt very close to being severed.

"Oh, ancestors," one of the elders whispered, as a breeze swept in with a concerned Guardian who now stood in the entryway. The slight breeze circled around Bode and the King, and as it swirled, the ashes of what was once King Obade were swept up into the air and scattered.

Bode watched, with no change in his expression until the last bits of the King faded, and then he coughed. Blood trickled from the corner of his mouth just as he started to fall to his knees. Arkean caught Bode in his arms before he hit the ground and they both dropped to their knees.

Screams shattered the silence as the Queen mother and her sister wives attempted to get into the room, along with several Guardians.

"Release your hold on me," the elder, the one who stood against them asked Arkean, cautiously.

More voices filled the space around them but Arkean shut them out, his focus remaining on his dying cousin and loving friend as he sent a mental call out to Quende and Gedgi.

"Let me go," Bode whispered.

"*Shhh.*" Arkean shook his head.

Bode coughed, spraying blood over Arkean's chest and face. "You are killing yourself by keeping me here. Let me go," Bode pleaded.

Arkean was draining himself but it wasn't by just keeping Bode alive. He was also keeping those not in the room out. He kept those still alive in the room away, and he was shielding the Four's mates and their loved ones from any possible attack. The King was dead, and dissension was imminent with his eldest and most powerful heir dying.

Some of the Guardians would see him, Quende, and Gedgi dead. Hate, combined with a Guardian's skill, intelligence, strength, and sometimes arrogance was a toxic mix of lethal unrest that will be hard to extinguish.

With the mood Arkean was in right now…extinguishing all the people who hated them was a real possibility for the usually diplomatic male.

Arkean felt a hand on his shoulder so he lifted his head to see Quende.

"Calm, Bode," Gedgi said as he peeled Bode's fingers from around the blade. "He is fading."

"Protect our kin and keep everyone out," Arkean told Quende.

Quende escorted the elders and the Guardians out of the room. "It is done," Quende said as he came back to stand near Arkean, Bode, and Gedgi a minute later.

Feeling Quende's and Gedgi's shields encompass the people dear to them all, Arkean finally released his own. With a sigh, he let his shields fall from close to a dozen Royal relations and other kin but kept his shield on their four mates.

Bode's eyes were glossed over now. "You will mate Mye, Arkean," he wheezed, "she is yet unspoiled." Bode coughed up more blood then took a deep breath. "Do not let her suffer as she has with no mate to care for…to love her."

Arkean only shook his head. He didn't trust his words would come out clear due to the thick burn of emotion swelling in his throat as Bode fought for each breath he took. "Mye will have you and no other," Arkean said. "Now still yourself." With a lightning quick movement, he pulled the dagger from Bode's chest and dropped it to the floor.

Bode's roar was loud and pain-filled as his chest jolted up. Arkean covered the wound quickly to lessen the blood loss. He closed his eyes and in doing so blocked everything and everyone out. He focused only on Bode, the slowing heartbeat and blood flow, the shallow breaths, and the chilling skin beneath his palm.

Arkean saw his life with Bode flash through his mind. He remembered the love he felt for Bode when he first saw the smiling boy in Cire's dwelling. He wanted nothing but to protect the devoted male who rarely left his side as a boy.

Arkean's thoughts then went to Lette in the cave. He saw the life in Lette's eyes dim as he gave what his planet held dear to four unknown males he had no choice but to trust to allow his people's legacy to live on. Arkean vowed that Lette and his people would live on.

The Ilterians will live on in all of us.

"I imagine this will hurt," Arkean winced. "I am sorry for that."

Hope lit in Bode's fading gaze. *"Are you capable of saving the dying?"*

Arkean smiled as Bode's thoughts flickered in his mind. *"I am capable of much, much more."*

Arkean knew there would be no turning back once he fully embraced the Coesen he was and the power he held bound inside him. But for one he loved, he would do anything.

Blinding light filled the room. Another pained scream shattered the silence.

13

Something is wrong.

That was Eyet's first thought when her eyes fluttered open. The room was dimly lit but her eyes still ached when she opened them. She had to blink several times before she could see clearly. She heard muffled speech and what sounded like moans and grunts outside the room she was…

Eyet looked down at herself then around the unfamiliar room.

She lay on very comfortable bedding that seemed made for a queen. Though she wanted to nestle deeper into the blankets and sleep more, her instincts were telling her to rise.

Arkean was hurting.

"What is happening?"

That voice was Ivi's. Eyet pushed up on her elbows first. Feeling stable, she swung her legs off the bedding, allowing her bare feet to touch the floor. Pushing off the bedding she toggled on her own two feet for a moment. She felt, but she also…knew that her body hadn't been used in some time. Yet, she felt no weakness. She was just a little unsure.

What she was sure of was that Arkean was in mental anguish.

More voices drifted to her.

"Let us pass Gedgi," Anis begged. "Can you not see how upset Mye is?"

"It is Arkean who has placed the barrier on the dwelling and on each of you. Even if I could remove it, which I cannot, I would not," Gedgi told them.

"We must go," Quende said. "Arkean needs us. You are all safe." His words sparked more unrest.

Eyet turned the corner on wobbly legs just as the two men left, leaving the gathered women in front of the entryway. She said nothing as the women talked amongst themselves but it was Mye who turned to her first. Her beautiful tear-streaked face was full of worry.

Eyet went to her with open arms. Somehow, Mye knew just as she did, just as all the mates of The Four did. Bode was mortally wounded.

Eyet folded Mye in her arms, holding her tight like a sister would.

●

The waiting was difficult. As the sun descended the women kept each other company. No one felt like doing much of anything. Neither of The Four returned with news and the women were still encased in a barrier, preventing them from leaving Arkean's dwelling.
Well…it was her dwelling too, now.

With mid-day meal forgotten, Cire took the lead and got the women cooking evening meal even though everyone was too worried to eat. Preparing the vegetables for the meal didn't take Eyet's mind off what was going on but it calmed her some. Especially since what she thought was a connection she felt to Arkean was suddenly severed. She suspected that was his doing.

Once she was done peeling and cutting, Eyet glanced around the courtyard at the women she loved as if blood-related. They weren't talking much but they worked in unison. Unlike Eyet, who was trained in the Bodai ways from an early age, Anis, who was pampered her entire life, even seemed to find her place and contributed among them.

There was one person missing among the women who gathered together.

Eyet found Mye sitting near the entryway looking out into…well, nothing. The barrier was one that distorted the view for those looking out and for whoever tried looking in as well.

Mye looked up at Eyet as if sensing her stare. The look on her face was utter hopelessness as she moved her hands to convey her words.

"He is shut off from me but I still feel him…I think," Mye signed then paused. She looked down for a moment, sighed then looked back up. *"I wanted for so long and received nothing. I got used to nothing."* A hint of a smile appeared on her lovely face. She truly was one of the most beautiful women Eyet ever saw. *"He chose me even though I am broken and… I wanted this,"* she signed, then touched her heart. *"I want how he makes me feel. I want him."*

Eyet walked over to where Mye sat and sank to the floor in front of her. "You are not broken Mye," Eyet said as she signed. "Bode chose you because you are a beautiful female with a beautiful spirit. He treasures you, he told me himself. I do not know what is going on out there but I know that Bode will fight to get back to you."

And Arkean will fight to make it so, Eyet said to herself.

●

It was the absence of sound that prompted Eyet to open her eyes. Rubbing them, she tried to remember when she walked to the room. She also realized that at some point she must have fallen asleep, even amidst her worry. That she may have done, but she did not remember changing her clothing or cleansing her body.

Eyet also felt…mentally refreshed.

How, she wondered as she did a full body stretch in her most comfortable new bed.

The room was lit from the glow of a single candle. It was enough light to make out the figure standing in the entryway watching her. She couldn't see his face because he stood in the shadows but Eyet knew it was Arkean.

Sitting up, she found it hard not to blush when she asked, "Did you…clean me?"

"I did."

It was a simple answer. Obviously, he felt no heat or flutters from seeing her, as she did from just the thought of him seeing or touching her. She inwardly cursed that she was so visibly affected by him but he was so closed off to her. She wanted a reaction from her mate but it seemed he may never show her the passion inside him.

With a sigh of acceptance, Eyet asked, "How long have I been asleep?"

He stood still and silent for so long she was uncertain if he would answer. Arkean lowered his head. "Mid-day meal has been eaten."

Mid-day meal…

That meant she slept through the night and half the next day. Panic replaced her refreshed thoughts, "Bode…Mye, where is she?"

"Calm. She is safe. I placed her and the other females in a healing sleep as well. You were all exhausted and ill with worry."

"And Bode… Does he breathe?" Eyet asked.

Arkean raised his gaze to her then lowered his head again.

She wished she could see his face and gauge what he was feeling, not that he would allow her to see much but just seeing his eyes were always a comfort to her. Since their first meeting.

"Bode breathes, but if he will ever be whole, I do not know. I fear the scars of the past day will forever be with him. With me," Arkean admitted. The last two words were a mere whisper. "The King is dead. There was no saving him. Once life leaves a body it is gone. I have no power to bring the dead back," he muttered. Arkean raised his head and spoke clearer. "Bode is with his kin. There are changes to come. He is advising them of their choices. I am here to advise you of yours."

"Mine?" Eyet had to tamper down her sadness over the King's death to focus on what Arkean was telling her now.

He exhaled, "Yes Eyet, you have a choice to make as well." Arkean took a step forward but stopped.

Eyet didn't think he would move closer but he sped forward, closing the distance so that he was a few inches from the bedding which she still lay upon. His head hung down so she was still unable to see his face. He was close enough to touch but she held steady.

With a slight motion of Arkean's hand, more candles were lit around the room. The room was illuminated so suddenly that Eyet had to blink several times to adjust to the change. When she did, it was Arkean's perfect form that she focused on.

The top half of his body was bare, aside from the jeweled bands around his neck and wrist. His lean muscled chest exposed every ripple and ridge to her appraising eyes. Before this day she never dared to openly stare at Arkean for fear of someone finding out how she felt.

Now…now they were mated and she could look her fill. Her eyes fell to his waist where his wrap hung off his hips, covering what she knew were two strong chiseled thighs. She could look at him for long spans of time and would have if the silence had not been so disturbing. She looked back up as Arkean sat on the bed beside her covered outstretched legs. His head was up but his eyes were still closed.

"I offer you the choice to withdraw from my claim on you," he said, his face stoic, but his voice trembled.

Withdraw?

It was a way to end a mating that did not benefit the female. By granting a withdraw, the female would leave the arrangement with grace and generally with her maidenhood intact. The male can re-mate but usually doesn't due to speculation and rumors that he was unworthy.

Did he change his mind about me?

How many nights did she lay awake thinking of Arkean and her together? Each day she woke her heart sank in the pit of her stomach as she worried that it would be the day that

Bode would go off to complete his Maatii and claim her while Arkean claimed another. And when they did leave for the Maatii, she was a shell of herself as she waited to be claimed.

Life with Bode would not have been so bad, she figured, but it would not have been…

She would not feel what she did since the moment Arkean drained his blood in her chalice. It was then that Eyet felt whole for the first time in her life. She felt sweet anticipation, immense happiness, and a yearning that threatened to burn right through her. Yet, now he wanted her to turn away from what promised to be a good life and smart match.

The weight of her sudden sadness made her feel limp. It was good she still lay on the bedding because she would have fallen if she were standing. The hurt she felt from hearing that one word "withdraw"' shattered her. Eyet felt dizzy, her mouth felt dry, and her heart drummed.

"You do not want me?" Eyet asked, her voice sounded thick and shaky.

She couldn't believe he didn't want her, but truly what proof did she have that he did want her, other than the word of a crazed Seer who wanted him all to herself? Lyar could have been wrong.

Desire? Maybe he desired her but he did not want her. And, why would he? Arkean was a proud Warrior who hated her people, her father. Why would he sully himself with her? The realization of it tore her in pieces.

He frowned. "It is you who may not want me." With that, Arkean opened his eyes.

Eyet sucked in a breath as she took in what she was seeing.

"Eyet, I can no longer ignore what I have become. It is clear to anyone who sees me that I am not who I once was."

Eyet unconsciously raised her hand toward his face but pulled back before touching him. Her wide eyes stared at him but there were no words to describe what she was seeing. The brown soulful eyes that she loved so much were no more. His pupils were black, but his eyes were now the color of a stormy gray sky.

"The Four cannot stay with the Bodai. Some fear how much we have changed," Arkean told her.

Eyet thought of the recent changes and the discussions that she and the other mates had about what they were experiencing. The elders had good reason to fear them if they could not see the benefit of these great Guardians.

"We have decided to start anew. But you were sent here to be a Bodai Queen, Eyet. You can still be that if you wish it. Bode has relinquished his claim to rule to his mother's eldest brother, the Guardian Bresi." Arkean stiffened when he said the rest. "Some Bodai have expressed that they would like to leave with us so it has been decided that everyone will be given a choice. Bresi and some of the elders feel that the choice should be given to each of our mates as well. He has made it clear that he wants you as his mate and Queen."

●

It took everything Arkean could muster not to rip Bresi's head from his body, but the Bodai Guardian and the elders who were advising him made a valid request. It was one that he would make as well if the situation were reversed. The situation was the way it was and he was presented with the task of presenting the choice to the one woman that he would rather die for than lose.

Arkean looked at Eyet through his newly transformed eyes. He hadn't seen the change for himself yet but he was aware that the change was significant by the way that everyone, including the three males closest to him, responded.

Bode, Quende, and Gedgi looked at him with admiration and awe. To them, who embraced Lette's legacy from the moment they received it, his new eye color was a symbol of the beings that were lost but whose future was forever intertwined with theirs. It was an honor to them, to have a visual reminder of the Ilterians.

The COESEN

The fact that he was the first to assist and accept Lette's gifts and legacy, but had resisted fully embracing the change would forever haunt him. He was a Guardian and a man of his word but his promise to Lette took a back seat to what he thought was his destiny. Being a Bodai Guardian who held the same greatness, devotion, and strength of his sire was all that mattered. He thought he could be a Guardian and still fulfill Lette's legacy but the truth was that the moment Lette entered their lives they were Bodai no more. They were now Coesen, two becoming one, and the only way to do what he promised Lette, to not let the Ilterians die, was to live as…and embrace the male he had become.

Coesen was what they were now and they decided to begin anew as such.

Eyet's hand hovered just in front of his eyes then she abruptly pulled it back. Her lips pursed as if she was going to say something then they softened. Her own eyes seemed confused one moment, unfocused as if in a trance, and then settled with a myriad of emotions. One of those emotions found its way to the surface and she spoke, projecting every bit of her frustration.

"I…I don't understand. Why do you offer this choice to me?" Eyet frowned. "Are we not mated? Do I not go where you go?"

Overcome with emotion, Arkean allowed himself to briefly feel what Eyet was feeling. Instead of fear or disgust, there was only…frustration. That simple emotion together with her facial expressions spoke volumes. His eyes didn't frighten her and it seemed that Eyet wanted to hold to their mating. It wasn't a declaration of love but he would take it, yet he still needed to warn her.

"I cannot ask you to endure what may come. You can have what you were meant to have here with Bresi."

It took him by surprise when her hand touched his face. Her palm was warm and soft and all he wanted to do was lean into her touch so he did. When she smiled, it literally took his breath away.

"You do not have to ask. I am your mate and I will remain so." Eyet lowered her head a bit but kept eye contact. "If it is what you will."

A need to claim his mate pulsed through Arkean. Gripping her wrist gently, Arkean pulled her hand from his face and placed it to his mouth to kiss. He felt her shudder with a sigh as he lowered her hand from his lips, leaned in, and trailed a string of light kisses along her jaw. Her breath hitched just when he reached her lips. Arkean paused just inches from claiming them.

"It is what I will. You are mine," he breathed, finally knowing it to be true.

"Then you must claim me in all ways," she said, breathlessly against his mouth.

Her hands hesitantly touched his chest then boldly moved up until she wrapped them around his neck. Arkean deepened the kiss as he moved the bed covers aside and slid over her as he slowly eased her down on the bedding. Using his arms to brace himself over her, Arkean moved his hand up the side of her body, feeling every soft curve.

Nothing in this world or beyond could possibly feel this good.

His mind was going to overload with the glorious sensations of touching his lips to hers while his hand explored her delicate body.

And the sounds that were coming from her tore at his control. It was a fight he would win because being gentle with Eyet was imperative. Like him, she was unspoiled, and he would die before causing her any unnecessary pain.

Breaking their connection, Arkean pushed up and began to remove Eyet's linen dress. Unclothing her was somewhat awkward but with her assistance, he managed. Disrobing himself was much easier and faster. When their bare bodies touched, melting onto the bedding, Arkean couldn't hold back the deep throaty moan that escaped him as he settled between her legs.

Eyet tensed with a grunt when he eased into her, crying out when her innocence broke away to accommodate his intrusion.

Arkean stilled, "I can take away the pain."

"No!" she grabbed his face in her hands. "I want to experience this with you the way it should be."

Understanding completely, Arkean kissed the tears on either side of her face with a softness he never knew he possessed. Then he carefully slid the rest of the way inside her, relishing in all her warm wetness until he could go no further. He knew he was big, her grimace and the strain on her face told him she was uncomfortable but she took what he gave with a determination that humbled him.

Breathing heavily, he asked, "You are well?"

She nodded. With her assurance, Arkean began a slow agonizing pace. Eventually, he felt the tension in her body thaw, allowing him the freedom to move a little faster, deeper. He could hardly contain the foreign sensations that filled him, and her growing moans of pleasure urged him on.

When her inner walls clenched around him, creating a most glorious pull, he angled himself so that he could drive inside her deeper. Eyet's cries quickened then she called out his name. That was when instinct took over. Arkean moved faster, his muscles tensed, his pleasure throbbed, and the need to release chased him to the very edge of sanity.

He released with such force that he thought his body burst into a million pieces.

Arkean continued to move to a slow rhythm as he buried his head in the crook of her neck to muffle his cry as pleasured moved through him. Eyet dug her nails into his back as she arched into him. Her mouth opened to let out a silent cry as her own release took hold of her, only finding her voice as the last of his seed spilled into her.

Bracing on his elbows so as not to put too much weight on Eyet, Arkean waited for his heart to resume its normal pace. It took even longer for his mind to settle. He had no words for what he was feeling. No way could he explain to her what she just gave him. All he could do was pull her to him and hold her close while he whispered how much he cared for her.

As Eyet's breathing leveled, she trailed her hand up and down his chest as she responded to his promises with her own. Eventually, he quieted and she hummed an Egyptian lullaby he vaguely recognized from his childhood.

Arkean's last thoughts before he fell asleep were of Bode.

●

"Mye, wake for me."

The voice in her head sounded pained and tired, yet to Mye it was all she needed to pull her from the dreamless sleep that took her. Her eyes sprang open to find Bode sitting beside her. She did a quick look around to see where they were. It was their dwelling.

She turned her attention back to him and her heart sank. Bode looked worn and defeated.

"*What happened*?" she asked, replacing her hand signals with mental communication.

"*I killed him. I killed my father,*" he transferred, sounding empty.

She had no idea where the tears came from. All she knew was they were falling like a rain shower from her eyes. His pain was so palpable she felt it coming off him as if it were her own. Somehow, she knew what happened. She knew how deep his pain ran, how regretful he was. Yet what shocked her most was how determined Bode was to save Arkean at all costs regardless of his own safety or the safety of anyone else in that room.

Mye lifted her hand to his chest where the dagger entered. She was whimpering now as she traced the spot that no longer showed any signs of damage.

Bode stiffened.

She lifted her gaze to his eyes. His brows lowered and his forehead creased then softened with understanding.

"Oh Mye," Bode transferred. He placed his hands over hers. *"I did not mean to project my pain on to you. If...I swear to you I had no idea that I could...that I was..."* He stopped mid-sentence and grabbed her face in his hands, looking into her eyes for several heartbeats before pulling her to him and embracing her.

A large amount of the pain, hurt, and sadness seemed to lift from her.

"I too am sorry," Mye transferred as she lay her head on his chest.

He released her then placed his finger under her chin. *"Better?"* Bode asked.

"Please," Mye transferred, *"I do not understand what just happened but please do not worry for me. I ask you to find a way to get past what has happened. To find something that will make you as happy and loving as you once were, because keeping this pain will harm you, Bode."*

His brows scrunched together as he watched her for a while. He looked confused as if he was working out things in his head. The smile he smiled was not one she was accustomed to seeing. It didn't reach his eyes but she would take it.

"I have you," Bode said. Before she could react, his lips were on hers.

"And I have you."

●

The day was clear and began so nicely that Eyet could not fathom the sudden change as she stepped out of her dwelling. She awakened in Arkean's arms, sore yet satisfied. The night was filled with his careful attention and when morn arrived he fed her like she was still royalty. She had never been as happy as she was now.

That was until they left the security that their dwelling provided her.

When they walked through the village, eyes followed them. It was nothing new. People always watched her come and go about her daily errands and Arkean always caught everyone's attention. He was a force that unknowingly drew in everyone around him. Though today the way the people watched them, it was not the awe she usually saw reflected in their eyes.

Worry was thick in the air as everyone walked to the center circle. Faces were sad and confused. Some looked worried, others seemed angry. And they all stopped whatever they were doing to watch her and Arkean pass.

Life was changing for them all. The unknown was scary. She felt saddened by the King's death; he was always kind to her but she couldn't help but embrace the buzz of excitement that fluttered in her belly. Eyet was on a new path with the one male she dreamed about.

"Are you well?"

Eyet turned to look over her shoulder at Arkean who was walking a few steps behind her. He still saw her as a Royal instead of his mate and equal, and that bothered her. She shook the confusion of his actions off and focused on him.

But behind Arkean, two Guardians followed, walking side by side. She didn't notice them before now and their presence startled her.

Arkean caught her arm to steady her as one of her feet tripped over the other. "Calm Eyet. They are here for your protection." He helped her stand straight. His eyes were on her but she could tell that he was aware of everything around them, probing for bad intentions.

She nodded once, then stepped into a walk as gracefully as she could. She did not know the circumstances behind King Obade's death but she understood everyone's caution. Arkean let her lead the way through the village until they approached the large ceremonial circle where most of the village's business was conducted. When the circle came into view he easily positioned his beautiful form in front of her. The gathering of people separated as they made their way through.

They walked into the circle and made their way to where the rest of The Four stood with their mates beside them. Eyet walked beside Arkean and came up to stand beside him when he stepped in next to the others.

Sitting on King Obade's throne above them was Bresi. He was a few Sumas older than Arkean and was a Guardian of great skill according to the villagers. He was handsome like most of the King's lineage and Bodai people. She saw him often. Bresi was a relative of Bode's but in what way she did not know. He peered at her with obvious interest and that made her a bit uncomfortable. She felt a burn in her cheeks as she looked away.

She let her gaze move over the other people in attendance. Several Guardians stood behind Bresi along with his mate and his mate's father.

"Have things been explained to the females?" Bresi asked, sounding confident and Kingly.

Bode stepped forward and bowed his head slightly, acknowledging and at the same time informing the crowd that Bresi was the undisputed King of the Bodai.

"Our mates," Bode said, emphasizing the word 'mates', "have been informed that they have a choice to make."

With that Bresi stood. He seemed larger now that he was standing. His whole demeanor was one of status as he set his eyes on Eyet then the other three mates.

"I offer you four women, a place here. You do not have to leave your home with these males. I know that any Guardian here will have you as a mate."

It seemed he meant his words for all of them but then he turned to her and Eyet frowned.

"I will make a good mate to you, Eyet. You would be Queen over all my mates and even my favored first wife."

The air seemed too thick for her to take in. She was told she would have to choose but now that the time was here it felt odd and wrong. Beside her, she could feel the anger that pulsed beneath Arkean's cool façade. Above her, on the throne platform, she saw the pain in Bresi's mate's eyes as she swallowed his words to take her position of head wife and newly crowned queen away. The crowd erupted in hushed conversation as they watched with interest.

Taking a deep breath Eyet did something no one ever did in public. She took Arkean's hand that was balled in a fist between them and slid her fingers between his. There was no rule about public expressions of love or intimacy but it was frowned upon so no one ever did it.

Relief rippled through her when Arkean's fingers locked around hers in a firm but gentle grip. It gave her the strength to speak. "I go where my mate takes me." Her voice was polite but firm with all the confidence she felt.

"I go where my mate takes me," Anis spoke up and added with confidence.

"I too go where my mate goes," Kya said with a smile.

Eyet looked over at Mye who was looking at Bode. Something was passing between the two then Mye broke eye contact with him and looked at Arkean pleadingly. Eyet felt Arkean's hand that embraced hers move, so she turned to Arkean who was now gently kissing her fingers. Heat burned from the simple kiss to travel through her hand and up her arm only to fade when he released her hand.

She watched as Arkean walked over to Mye.

"The changes…you have noticed?" Arkean asked.

Mye nodded.

"The damage is slowly repairing itself but if you wish it, I can help."

Mye's eyes began to tear and her chest rose and fell with deep breaths.

Bode didn't speak but Eyet could see he was trying hard to remain still and calm.

Mye nodded again.

Eyet watched as Arkean looked at Bode for a moment then smiled when Bode gave a slight nod. Arkean placed his hand over Mye's throat.

Mye sucked in a hissing gulp of air then coughed. All the noise, of nature and man, seemed to silence around them. Eyet watched transfixed as Mye sucked in another gulp of air, hummed a shaky sound then spoke words for the first time in her life.

"I…I go. I go where…my mate. Takes me," Mye said as tears spilled from her eyes.

The people standing around seemed to explode with emotion and conversation. Some cursed them and others shouted with praise. Bresi seemed shocked and somewhat upset, then his eyes focused on Eyet again and she saw what can only be described as disappointment. Had he always wanted her and she just didn't notice?

"He has," Arkean said quietly as he moved to stand beside her.

Eyet looked over at her mate, her brows furrowed with confusion. "Are you reading my thoughts?"

He faced her and spoke in a low voice. "I haven't used my abilities as often as the rest so I have not mastered a way to close off from one when I listen to others. It is like every inner voice in the world is speaking at the same time. Yours is the one I find the most calming. I mean no harm. I ask that you forgive my intrusion but I need to know what these men are thinking so I will be prepared."

Eyet smiled and wanted to kiss him because she saw the strain of such a gift reflected in his eyes, but them holding hands and a miracle was enough for the Bodai to handle today.

"I wish I could lessen your worries."

"You do every time you look at me," he said with a smile.

She was about to throw caution to the wind and kiss her mate when Bresi's voice boomed out over the crowd.

"Calm all," he bellowed. He set his now-hardened gaze on her then slowly swept it over the lot of them. "You women have made your choice," he said then sighed. "No one will stop you as you take your leave." He then sat down on his throne and waited for them to go.

Eyet was moving her feet to do just that when she noticed that Arkean and Bode were not moving. She glanced over to Quende and Gedgi who were still firmly in place.

"They are using the mind talk again," Anis said in her ear.

That is when Eyet realized the women gathered around her.

"Be still and stay with the women," Arkean spoke in her head. *"You all are protected."*

Anis and the other women nodded. They must have received the same words from their mates.

"We have offered our mates a choice," Arkean spoke over the crowd, "Now you will offer that same choice to the other Bodai."

Bresi straightened on the throne. He shook with anger as his words came out, "I offer nothing to them. They are my people now," he spat, "not yours. I am King. I am their leader. You will leave this place now."

Arkean sighed, suddenly looking tired. When he spoke, Eyet could tell he would use force if need be.

"We will not go until we know if others desire to go with us. It is their right. The Bodai Tribe is done. It died when Bode gave you the throne. These people are not tied to the Bresi Tribe yet. They are free to choose where they will settle. It is their right." Arkean rolled his neck and stood straighter. "Do not force my hand on this Bresi. You will not like the outcome," he said calmly.

Too calmly for Eyet's liking.

Bresi seemed to think this over for a moment then shrugged. "I doubt any of them will leave with you," he sneered, "but as a male of worth, I will make the offer." Bresi smiled a knowing smile as if he knew the thoughts of all the people. "Anyone who wants to leave your home to go with these *men* should step forward."

There was no hesitation when Bresi's last word came out. "I will go," a familiar voice called out.

It took a moment for Cire to navigate through the crowd but when she did she came to stand with them. Ivi spoke next, her young voice lifting above the crowd's as she informed them she too was leaving.

This didn't bother Bresi. Neither did the calls that came from some other relatives of the Four. Eyet figured Bresi knew that close family might stick with them. What he wasn't happy with was the number of Guardians and women that slowly trickled forward. It began with one of the Guardians who escorted them. Then the other Guardian who escorted them spoke up.

Their coming forward sparked something in the crowd. By the time silence reigned there were more than fifty Guardians and thirty men and boys who stepped forward. What surprised everyone was that more than forty females also decided to break from the new Bresi Tribe.

Some were mated to the men or the offspring of one or two who already spoke their choice to leave, but many were young girls who were coming into their womanhood and would be ready to mate soon. With the men to women ratio in the village, this was a devastating blow to Bresi and his leadership.

"You can take with you the Guardians, the common men, and their mates who chose to go but I cannot allow the blossoming females to leave with you." Bresi was standing now. The tick in his jaw might be a permanent condition now.

Calmly, Arkean said, "It is their choice to make. Not mine, not yours."

"Females have no choice," Bresi said. His words dripped with arrogance and an unspoken challenge.

Eyet knew that it would come to this when so many came forward. She hoped that things would go smoothly. That

Arkean and his brethren would suffer no more this day other than leaving their home for the unknown. But it wasn't to be.

"My great-mother is a female and I treasure her words as I do the words of my Prince." Arkean glanced over at Bode.

Bode accepted his admission with a slight smile and a nod. He apparently felt the same way.

Eyet found their silent communication somewhat unnerving but it was who they were now. Even before the change, the two seemed to silently share things.

"The women will decide their path," Arkean said.

"No!" Bresi shouted. "Females. Decide. Nothing. They will stay here…with us. I cannot allow you this."

Of course, Bresi would disagree. If the females left it would deplete their mating age female numbers to almost half.

"You will. The females are not mated. They decide. You have no say in this." To further his point, Arkean turned to the women in question and asked them. "To leave with us, is this what you all want?" A combined though shaky "yes" filled the silence. "Then that is what will happen," he assured them.

Arkean stilled and tilted his head toward the throne. With blinding speed, Arkean moved before Bresi could speak the words that must have formed in his mind. It was clear to all that Bresi was going to issue an attack.

The new King fell back onto his throne with a shocked expression on his face as he peered up at Arkean. The Guardians at the throne were tense but none moved to remove Arkean from the raised platform that was meant only for the King, Queen, and close royals and their guards.

●

Arkean's words were quiet and held a patience he didn't feel, but they projected calmly out over the crowd. "I know you are a well-brought-up male Bresi. You have never treated me ill so I will dismiss the thoughts in your head."

The new King could not stop thinking of Eyet naked, beneath him. Arkean knew his mate was beautiful and many admired her as he did. The knowledge that Bresi would never have her comforted him…so the new King could live.

"But know that if you order these males to attack us, to harm what I hold dear…then know that none of you will survive.

"What happened last eve was a mishap. It was not done in anger but our King…my kin is no more because I was unable to see that nothing is what it once was."

Unable to resist, Arkean glanced at Bode to see that the pain of losing his father in such a way would never ease. He would never be able to express how deeply sorry he was, but he needed to deal with what was at hand now before he had to shed more blood.

"I failed them but I will not now. So be careful what you say," Arkean whispered his next words in Bresi's mind, "*and what you think.*" Speaking out loud again, Arkean finished, "because if I feel that you mean to harm them I will strike before you even give the order."

"Wh…why do you speak for them?" Bresi stammered.

"He speaks for us because he is our King," Bode said with a genuine smile.

Arkean looked over his shoulder to see Bode, Quende, and Gedgi lower their heads to him as a gesture of respect. There was a collective gasp from the crowd but Arkean's eyes fell on Eyet, who gave him a slight smile then bowed her head. The mates of the Four followed suit.

Arkean felt such pride that he blinked a few times. But he turned his attention back to Bresi. "We are all Kings but every nation needs someone to be at the head. They chose me to be that figure. Do we understand each other now, Bresi?"

Bresi's eyes sliced through Arkean with contempt and fear, but there was acceptance in them as well. He managed a slight nod of his head.

Arkean stepped off the high platform, landing softly on his feet with the grace of a sleek feline as he gazed over the people who put their trust in him and his friends to keep them safe. "We will meet at midday meal at my dwelling to plan our journey." The crowd thinned as some people dragged themselves back to their daily life while Arkean's group sort of lingered.

The Four spoke of what needed to be done. They went over all possible scenarios and the outcomes concerning their departure and relocation. The change in their mates was also discussed in detail. Each of them not only carried a mark just behind their left ear but had a significant increase in their sensory abilities. The women's bodies were also changing, almost as if any damage they had was slowly repairing itself and they were becoming stronger.

"If our blood could help others like it helped our mates," Quende said as if he was speaking his thoughts.

Gedgi frowned. "I worried that Anis would not survive. Hetu is young still. She may not come through like the others have."

Arkean listened quietly and said nothing for several seconds. Before he spoke he looked to Bode who remained mostly silent throughout most of the meeting. It was evident that he was partially there and partially somewhere else. Yet, Bode was listening and gave him a subtle nod. The cousins did know each other well.

Arkean spoke, "We need them all to be strong for the journey. Our blood can make them strong. If they will have it we will give it."

Bode, Gedgi, and Quende all nodded at once.

As Arkean and his Counsel made their way back to his dwelling, he knew his decision to share their blood was the right thing to do. He and his Council remained behind to inform Bresi that they would be staying the night then leaving midday the next morning. That gave them time to prepare. When they reached his property, their entire group was waiting with the belongings they were taking with them.

"You found your place cousin. You are a born leader," Bode smiled as he placed a hand on Arkean's shoulder.

Arkean looked over at Bode. "As are you. I accept my role in the front but if I am right, we four will each reign." He stepped forward and addressed his people, explaining what he and his Council were offering them. Arkean advised them of what the blood did for their mates and that anyone who did not want to accept their gift could decline and still be accepted as a Coesen.

It came as no surprise that Cire, Ivi, and Gedgi's mother and sister Hetu were the first to accept. All the Guardians accepted their blood as well. Most of the males, boys, and half the females stepped forward for the offering. Everyone else expressed that they were willing to go but not sure about the blood offering.

The people who would be accepting the three drops of blood were split into four groups, determined by their relationship to each of The Four. Anyone related to one of The Four was placed in his group and offered his blood and no others. For the people who were not related, they were split evenly.

The process was easy. Each of the four cut a small slit in one of their fingers and allowed only three drops per person. Because it was less than what their mates took in, Arkean was sure they would not suffer the long sleep. When the offering was done, the women began the evening meal while the men talked about the journey to come.

It was their first meal together as Coesen, eaten on Arkean's property away from the newly named Bresi tribe. After the meal, everyone settled in for the night while Arkean and Bode took watch.

●

Morn came soon enough. Arkean helped Eyet and Cire gather their things then they waited at the wall while he scanned everyone's thoughts in the village, ready to send out a mental command to his friends or the Guardians who aligned with them if Bresi wanted to make trouble.

When everyone who was to accompany them arrived, they set off while the people they once would have died for, watched in silence.

Arkean had the perfect place to settle in mind. He led the way to where Lette's downed air machine crashed. The land was inhospitable but he and his brethren could manipulate the landscape to make it livable and hidden from the world. There were many things to discuss, like rules the Coesen would need to live by, but that could wait until they arrived at their new home.

He held comfort in the fact that he would not rule alone. Each of The Four will rule.

The marking of the people worked just as he thought. Even the ones who opted out of the first offering came to him during morn meal saying that they changed their minds and wanted the offering. Seeing that the others were healthy now was the deciding factor, plus the little fact that none of the original group turned ill or slept like the mates of the Four during transition.

Now every man, women, and child were branded with one of four marks. No one other than the Four showed signs of any mental abilities; the others showed only sensory and health-related changes and Arkean didn't think they would develop anymore.

But he was hopeful the children born to their new nation would.

The Coesen were their own people and follow their own laws. They will only mate with other Coesen, integrate with the outside lands only when necessary, and above all else, they decided to keep the knowledge of their gifts to themselves.

A sense of wholeness finally came over Arkean as he walked with Eyet, hand in hand. He mated the woman of his dreams and she cared deeply for him. Lette and his people will live on in them. For the first time in his life, Arkean felt as if he was going home.

With that in mind, Arkean smiled as he led his mate, his kin, and their people to their new land.

THE END
is Only the Beginning

Find out more about the Coesen in
The Binding of the Halo series
Excerpt Below…

Present Time

The door to suite 12-1 was already open when Tristan stepped off the elevator. The hotel clerk told him there would be someone to greet him. There wasn't.

When he slowly entered the room he half expected to see Zeta or the nameless young man who had come to Cianne's house a few days ago. Instead he saw Vivian, seated in the sitting area looking as regal as any queen.

She was fully dressed in an ankle length dark blue long sleeve dress, as if it were four in the afternoon versus four in the morning. He closed the door behind him and walked over to where she sat. She motioned for him to sit on the sofa across from her.

Tristan decided to stand. *Just in case.* "I think that I may be losing my mind," he said as he looked down at his feet then nervously rubbed his hand over his head. "I…uh, I can hear her in my head."

Vivian tilted her head to peer up at him with a look of shock on her face.

"I don't really know why I came here," Tristan said, "I just…" He rubbed his temples. "I was sitting in her room and I heard her whisper to me. At first, I thought it was just my mind replaying the things she's said to me before, you know, but—"

"What did she say?" Vivian moved to the edge of the chair, giving him her full attention.

"She said that…" he started then paused, as he sat down across from Vivian, "that she hoped the baby had my smile. That she loved my smile." He cleared his throat. Tristan looked at his hands then said what he came to say. "I know that you're different, like Cianne. Whenever you're around I feel, I feel like I must…I don't know." He shook his head. "That I must submit to you." He looked at Vivian. "I want you to tell me if she's…"

Tristan sighed and looked away. He was unable to finish the question he drove here to have answered.

"You want to know if she is dead and if it is her spirit you hear." Vivian sat back when he gave her a mournful nod. She then took her time inspecting him. "How do you feel Tristan?"

Tristan, puzzled by the question, frowned. He knew what the question meant, but he didn't know what she meant by asking the question.

"Let's try this then," Vivian said impatiently. "Zeta." Before Vivian finished saying the girl's name, a blur of color filled Tristan's field of vision. The petite one called Zeta was at Vivian's side.

In sync with Zeta's lightning speed entrance, Tristan went on alert and flipped over the sofa to a standing position in back of it. He quickly read the room for the other escort but only the girl was there. He relaxed only when he realized that she was not going to move until she was told.

Tristan looked at Vivian who was still seated on the sofa. She had a look on her face that made him very uneasy. He wasn't sure if it was a look of admiration or contempt.

"Sit down Tristan," Vivian said; serenity had returned to her face.

He hesitated briefly before sitting.

"You are a definite anomaly."

Tristan was tired of being insulted by the woman. First, he was an abomination and now an anomaly. His look of confusion was replaced by one of annoyance.

"Have you always moved with the reflexes and agility of a cheetah and with the strength of an elephant?

Again, she had him confused.

"You come from good stock dear, I've checked…but not that good," Vivian said shrewdly. When she realized she was going to get nothing but a glare from him, she continued, "You have been improved Tristan, upgraded. Some would say, perfected. I bet you were always the best at everything, right?"

He was always fast. It wasn't until a few seasons ago while playing football that he realized he was much faster than the other players. He was so fast that he had to make an effort to slow down and take a few hits to keep the crowds interested. But that was just the way he was. He had always been what coaches called exceptional, for as long as he could remember.

"You've been checking up on me?" Tristan asked calmly. From the moment he met her, he sensed that Vivian felt some way about him, but to insult his family was rude. Yet, she had the answers he needed. "Why?"

"At present, time is brief so you will get the short version of what has to be done. The full tutorial will have to wait. As for your original question, yes…Cianne lives." Vivian sighed as if bored. "Zeta will explain some things to you," she said then stood, "and then she is going to tell you how to find my granddaughter." Vivian started out of the room.

Tristan's eyes followed her as she proudly walked by him. There was no way she could have known how to find Cianne and hadn't told him. "You knew how to find her all this time," he accused, his voice shrill.

Vivian stopped. At first it seemed as if she would turn back and respond but she said nothing as she started out of the room again with her head held high.

"It's complicated, Tristan." A quiet voice came from beside him. "…and it is not our place to question." Her words were slow and precise with a subtle French accent.

Tristan looked over at the small girl who now sat beside him. He didn't even hear her move.

She reminded him of an adorable little devil. Just days ago, he was defending himself and now the girl who attacked him was being nice. Tristan moved over an inch, in case the sweet little angel decided to show her claws again.

"Complicated," Tristan sneered. His anger simmered. "If there is a way to find Cianne then I need to know now."

"I will tell you all I know but you need to listen to everything I have to say," Zeta insisted. "We…you and I, aren't like other people. Well," she said, smiling, "you are even more…special."

"What are you talking about?" Tristan's anger hadn't defused but he would listen, for now.

Zeta gave him an unreadable look, "Considering recent circumstances, and the fact that your Coesen was suppressed when she was just a little girl," she said, the last words slower than the rest as if she were thinking out loud. "We don't exactly know when she transferred to you. Your speed and strength have been seeping out just as her abilities have. That could be the explanation for why you didn't notice any changes in yourself."

Zeta lost him somewhere around the word Coesen. "My Coesen?" he asked, confused, "what circumstances?"

"Tristan," she said with excitement, "you are truly remarkable."

She held his gaze longer than Tristan felt comfortable, as if he was some kind of lab experiment.

"Vivian, as you call her, is the Sovereign of a race of exceptional humans. We are known as the Coesen. We can trace our lineage to four amazing men. You are what we call a Protector. You are your Coesen's physical defense against any and all aggressors. You will be stronger and faster than the average person and most other things in this world. You will think and react faster than any middling or the fastest animals.”

Tristan took a moment to process what Zeta told him. As farfetched as it all sounded, he knew that what she said was the truth. He *was* different, had always felt it. “What is a middling?”

“A middling is an average person without unique abilities. Your parents, Mr. Baxter, they are considered middlings,” she explained. “You are connected to your Ward. Protectors can always locate their Wards, the Coesen who has transferred the gift to them.”

Tristan considered this. “A guardian of sorts,” he said. “Then Cianne is…”

“She is a Coesen,” Zeta said slowly, for his benefit. “Was there ever a time when you felt overheated or warm when Cianne was near?”

Tristan thought back to all those times that he felt hot when they were in close proximity. “Yes,” he admitted. He thought that warmth was because she made him that nervous.

“That was the synching process your bodies were going through,” Zeta explained.

“Then what’s wrong with me?” Tristan asked. “If we are synched then why haven’t I got a clue as to where Cianne is? And if there are others like you, who can do things, then why haven’t your people found her yet?”

Zeta cleared her throat. “I don’t know,” she admitted, “but as her Protector, you are our best hope. As for you not being able to find her, we think it’s because her abilities are bound…and perhaps because you two are lovers.” She looked down nervously when Tristan met her gaze. “We think that because of your emotional connection to your Ward, you cannot focus properly…but we can’t be sure.”

“So, no Protector has ever been in love with their…” Tristan couldn’t remember the name. He was tired and still very angry.

"Coesen," she reminded him as she looked away.

Tristan waited for an answer as he stared at her profile. After a moment of silence, Zeta looked at him then nodded. Wards, sovereigns, supernatural powers, Tristan had no time to be amazed about what he learned. All he wanted was to know how it all would help him get Cianne safely back in his arms.

"Little is known of the two relationships similar to yours but both unions ended in death. Any such union would be looked at as an—"

"An abomination," Tristan finished.

"Unlawful," Zeta corrected. "The thing is, your love for her may be clouding your senses but you are, as I said before, not a 'normal' Protector. Mainly that is because Cianne, as you call her, isn't a "normal" Coesen." Zeta hesitated then said, "Mr. Baxter has informed us that she has been having visions. You are stronger and faster than most middlings, meaning your abilities are somewhat present, even though they shouldn't be. Cianne is very powerful. Her abilities were bound when she was a child, but apparently, they seem to be trickling out on their own which is enabling you use of the entitlement she has given you. Understand that once her abilities are unrestrained, once her power is fully released, yours will be significantly enhanced as well. The scope of what you two are capable of is… Well, it is unknown."

"It's Zeta, right?" Tristan asked. She nodded. "All that's exciting but I need to know what I can do now. If my feelings for her are clouding my senses, then what do I need to do to find her?"

"No Coesen has had the ability to hear anyone's thoughts for some time. If you are hearing her, as you say you are, then she may be able to hear you as well," Zeta said.

"I said that I *think* I *may* be hearing her." He wasn't sure anymore. He wasn't sure of anything.

The COESEN

A low buzzing sound alerted Tristan of a text message. He immediately pulled out his phone. His pulse increased. Finally.

Available Now

About The Author

Shea is a woman in love with the idea of love so it's no wonder she writes Romance Novels. The East Coast native is a romantic to her core and reads and watches anything with a love story. She especially likes binging on Romance TV around Christmas time.

She enjoys meeting people and chatting, collecting Barbie dolls, toys, anime, and is addicted to The Sims games. Shea also loves music and has mentioned that she writes better when she has movie scores playing as white noise in the background.

This new and exciting author writes Adult Romance in the sub-genres of Contemporary, New Adult, Paranormal, Sci-Fi, and Erotica. Come…Taste A Sample.

Shea Swain
The Pulse of Provocative Romance

Head on over to my website www.Sheaswainwrites.com for
Upcoming Releases,
Character Dream-casting

IF YOU LIKED THIS BOOK SIGN UP FOR MY NEWSLETTER
http://bit.ly/1JaAmmf
THANK YOU
and
Please consider leaving a review!

The COESEN

Heaven on Hell Island Blurb

If Bleu St. James relied on her first impression of Chris, she might have let him drown. But there is something about him that inexplicably draws her in. Maybe it was something she saw when she stared at his calm face as the plane they were on fell from the sky. Now stranded on a mysterious deserted island, Bleu must not only contend with the elements, she must depend on a survivalist who also happens to be a hate-filled extremist.

Chris Stokes can't keep his eyes off the well-dressed woman, even though he was taught that her kind is beneath him. Her very presence makes him feel inadequate in every way. Yet, Bleu saved his life and he owes her. That means doing his damnedest to keep her alive. Only, Chris can't deny how alluring Bleu is or how badly he wants her to see *him*, and not the man he no longer wants to be.

This book contains some views and language that may be uncomfortable for some. This story is about change, growth, and is for adults 18 years and older. Readers discretion advise.

Excerpt

Chapter 1

Dulles Intl. Airport
International flight 4816
Departure Gate 23

April 8th

Her

BLEU LIFTED HER DARK sunglasses above her eyes and glared at the two men who sat in the seats facing hers. A gentleman who looked to be of Middle Eastern descent just hurried away after a brief discussion with them. Now they were discussing the "problems" in the United States, rather loudly. Of course, the problems were due to everything and everyone else.

She didn't spare them much more than a glance and was about to focus on the magazine she just bought from the newsstand when one of them spoke to her.

"What the fuck are you looking at, Dark Meat?" It was the one whose head was completely shaved except for a long flop of blond hair that covered one of his eyes.

Bleu smirked as she raised her perfectly arched brow at him. They stared at each other for several seconds before she got bored, lowered her glasses, then stood.

She heard Flop-Over say something about hoity-toity dark meat to his friend, a guy who clearly loved tattoos. Their laughter followed her as she found another seat closer to the boarding gate.

As she took a seat that faced away from them, she thought, *Now I won't be able to see or hear the conversation of Neanderthals.*

Him

"What the fuck are you looking at, Dark Meat?" Thomas asked the black woman sitting across from them.

Chris watched her with curiosity, wondering what her response would be. Why he gave a fuck, he wasn't sure. Yeah, for a darky, the chick was hot. He'd seen a good number of black women he could admit were good looking but he never felt an inkling of interest in them.

But her…

Her skin was smooth and reminded him of warmed walnuts. Her hair was sleek and black, cut short all around but it was long enough in the front that she had to sweep it to the side. Her clothing, a very white shirt, and khaki long shorts, looked brand new. He was certain her sparkling stud earrings were real diamonds. Even her sunglasses looked like they cost more than his monthly rent. Her scent–*the Gods probably didn't smell half as good*–was intoxicating.

She probably has a "Sugar Daddy".

When she raised her brow at Thomas, briefly allowing Chris to see her dark seductive eyes, then smirked, Chris couldn't help but laugh to himself. Thomas and the chick competed in a stare off for several seconds before she lowered her glasses and stood.

Chris watched her walk…no, stroll away.

Some of them darkies pull you in, Chris. It's how they were made. To tempt the better races.

Chris closed his eyes in an attempt to purge his father's words from his head.

"Hoity dark meat needs to be put in her place," Thomas sneered as she walked away. "Don't know if I want to choke her with my hands or my cock."

"Sara will cut your shit right off," Chris responded. He intentionally sounded bored with the whole situation, as if he had little interest in *Her*.

Thomas laughed.

Chris absently joined in but he continued to watch *her*.

Her

Bleu glared at the *Fasten Seatbelt* sign that flashed above her head as the plane shook violently, jostling the passengers from side to side. Several overhead compartments burst open, spilling luggage onto the passengers. She leaned her head out into the aisle and saw two flight attendants who were strapped into their seats. Bleu wasn't comforted by the looks they gave each other before undoing their seat belts and rushing to assist a couple who were bombarded with the luggage.

The sheer panic expressed on their faces shocked Bleu into a silent prayer. She almost felt guilty for not going to church in over five years but that feeling passed with the next series of brutal shaking and shifting of the airplane.

When the aircraft suddenly dipped, Bleu saw one of the attendants grab a passenger for support. The other attendant flew up, crashed into the ceiling of the plane, then fell to the floor. Until now, the passengers seemed to make an effort to remain calm, just as the attendants requested. But now, screams and gasps filled the cabin. No one was buying that this was just turbulence anymore.

"Carla," the attendant's voice bellowed above the screaming.

But Carla, the other attendant, didn't answer. She looked unconscious.

Bleu closed her eyes. Her fingers ached from the death grip she had on the armrest of her seat. Her rigid posture was the only tell that she was scared to death. Her breathing was steady, and if she had a mirror she would see that her face reflected a calm she didn't feel. She trained her entire life to put her best face forward, to never let anyone know what she felt or thought.

What was she thinking right now?

She was thinking that she and every passenger on this plane was going to die. It was that simple. Bleu had flown a million times before so she knew that this was different. The other passengers knew it too.

Oddly, she had the silliest thought. *You don't know any of these people you're about to die with.*

With her stoic mask on, Bleu couldn't help her perusal of the frightened faces of her fellow passengers. They were all strangers. Bleu shut out the calls for help and the shouts to God as she looked over her shoulder to her left, at the pair from earlier who sat in seats across the aisle, one row behind hers.

Why she looked at the two men, she didn't know. Both had an air of danger about them but with Bleu's sheltered upbringing, even the postman seemed a bit nefarious. She grasped on to the fact that these men weren't *complete* strangers like the others aboard the flight. Maybe that was why she chose to seek them out.

Bleu recalled the brief, albeit annoying encounter she had with them right before boarding the airplane.

Now I'm going to die with these Neanderthals, she thought.

"*Dying is dying,*" Nana's disembodied voice whispered to her. "*It makes no never mind who you travel to the pearly gates with. Just be happy you made it.*"

Nana, Bleu thought with a sigh as the noise around her increased to deafening levels.

The sounds of screams, hushed prayers, and useless instructions filled the airplane cabin. The freak storm came about so suddenly, Bleu figured that there was nothing anyone could do. Their collective prayers were enough to raise the roof but sadly they weren't capable of saving them as lightning struck the back end with an ear-piercing boom.

Bleu covered her ears as she squeezed her eyes shut. The loud explosion overshadowed all other sounds around her. She managed to hold her scream in but her breathing picked up and her heart raced.

Available Now

The COESEN

191

www.ingramcontent.com/pod-product-compliance
Lightning Source LLC
Chambersburg PA
CBHW070651100726
47907CB00007B/2177